# THE LEWTON EXPERIMENT

 RACHEL SA

# THE LEWTON EXPERIMENT

 RACHEL SA

VANCOUVER   LONDON

Distribution and representation in Canada by
Fitzhenry & Whiteside • www.fitzhenry.ca

Distribution and representation in the UK by
Turnaround • www.turnaround-uk.com

Published in the UK and the US in 2013

**Mixed Sources**

Cert no. SW-COC-001271
© 1996 FSC

**FSC**

Inside pages printed on FSC certified paper using vegetable-based inks.

Manufactured by Sunrise Printing
Manufactured in Vancouver, BC, Canada in October 2012

2 4 6 8 10 9 7 5 3 1

Cataloguing-in-Publication Data for this book
is available from The British Library.

Library and Archives Canada Cataloguing in Publication

Sa, Rachel
The Lewton experiment / Rachel Sa.

ISBN 978-1-896580-97-5

I. Title.

PS8637.A15L49 2012          jC813'.6          C2012-902149-0

*The lyrics of 'Outside the Stars' used by kind permission of N. Q. Arbuckle and Six Shooter Records. All rights reserved by copyright holder.*

*The publisher wishes to thank*
*Anouk Moser and Arushi Raina for their editorial assistance.*
*The publisher also wishes to thank Rosemary Hall for her help.*

*Tradewind Books thanks the Governments of Canada and British Columbia for the financial support they have extended through the Canada Book Fund, Livres Canada Books, the Canada Council for the Arts, the British Columbia Arts Council and the British Columbia Book Publishing Tax Credit program.*

 Canada Council
for the Arts

Conseil des Arts
du Canada

 BRITISH COLUMBIA
ARTS COUNCIL
Supported by the Province of British Columbia

 Canadä

 LIVRES CANADA BOOKS

## DEDICATION:

For Bruce Kirkland, who has been here for the entire wild ride.

And in memory of Sherri Wood, who should have been.


## ACKNOWLEDGEMENTS:

I am eternally grateful to my diligent editors, R. David Stephens and Michael Katz, and to Glen Huser for his guidance and support.


## THANK YOU:

To the founders of the Muskoka Novel Marathon, for providing me the first opportunity to write this story;

To Anne Millyard, whose early enthusiasm spurred me on;

To Susan Juby, for her insights and valuable suggestions;

To Guy Allen, for always pushing my writing to the next level;

To Neville Quinlan and NQ Arbuckle for the music;

To Andrew Gray, Nancy Lee, my instructors and all of my classmates and friends at the University of British Columbia's Optional Residency Creative Writing program, for their support and inspiration.

# CHAPTER ONE

**WHEN SHERRI FIRST SET EYES ON THE DILAPIDATED BUS STATION** in the town of Lewton, the little hairs on her arms stood on end and a familiar thrill of curiosity stirred inside her. Her reporter radar told her trouble was coming. It never failed to send up a signal flare when there was a story to uncover.

Her boyfriend, Michael, liked to tease her that maybe it meant she was psychic, like she knew something bad was going to happen. But Sherri didn't buy all that hocus-pocus stuff.

"Lewton, all passengers for Lewton." The bus driver's voice crackled through the speakers overhead as the Greyhound rattled to a stop in the gravel parking lot. Sherri set down her dog-eared copy of *Jane Eyre* and peered out.

It didn't look like anyone had stopped here in a long time. Thorny weeds shot up through the crumbling pavement. A lone weather-beaten bench sat beneath a dangling sign that read: WELCOME TO LEWTON. But the 'w' and the 't' in the sign were so faded that it looked like she had just arrived in Leon.

Sherri's curiosity eclipsed her twinge of disappointment at the ramshackle look of the place. Jumping up from her cramped seat, she strode toward the front of the bus. She felt the eyes of the other passengers on her back. The driver had already bounded down the steps and out into a deserted parking lot. She caught up to him just as he hefted her giant pink suitcase onto the cracked pavement.

Sherri had expected a quaint bus station in the middle of a bustling tourist town. This was the beginning of summer, after all.

"Excuse me?" she asked. "What's up with this place?"

"It's Lewton." The driver shrugged, slamming the luggage compartment shut and straightening up. "Someone coming to meet you, miss?"

"My great aunt should be here any minute."

"That's good. Not many taxis come this way anymore," the driver said, ambling back toward the bus doors. "I can't remember the last time I had a passenger stop at Lewton. I keep expecting Greyhound to take Lewton off the northern route. Have a nice day."

The doors slammed shut. Sherri stepped back and watched the bus disappear down the lonely two-lane road. That's when she remembered her book.

"Damn, I left *Jane Eyre* on the bus!" Sherri hefted her backpack over her shoulder and dragged her heavy suitcase toward the splintered wooden bench. She glanced at her watch: 8:30 p.m. She was fifteen minutes late, but there was no sign of Aunt Gillian or anyone else. Sherri dug into her purse for her cellphone. No bars. *Great.* She glanced around for a payphone. No luck.

Sherri thought back to all the articles she'd read online about Lewton. They had all described it as a picturesque little town on the shores of Otter Lake crammed with antique shops, ice cream parlours and all the kinds of things tourists from the city loved about small towns. It sounded like the perfect place to be a student reporter for the summer.

Sitting down on the bench, Sherri pulled out a brochure she had picked up earlier at a little greasy spoon where the bus had stopped. WELCOME TO THE TOWN OF LEWTON—A GEM IN THE HEART OF MUSKOKA. A GREAT PLACE FOR FAMILIES! On the cover was a photo of a beaming family walking down what looked like Main Street—a mom and a dad holding the hands of their little, blonde twin girls. Sherri's reporter radar kicked in again. There was something off about the picture. They looked too perky.

Then Sherri took out another brochure: THE BERRY GROVE BED AND BREAKFAST. It looked much more inviting. This was Aunt Gillian and Uncle Walter's place, where she would be staying for the summer. The photo on the cover showed a pristine three-storey farmhouse with a wide shady porch wrapping around the front, and a two-person swing hanging near a screen door. Flower boxes bursting with lavender decorated the windows, and a giant weeping willow dominated the yard. It looked absolutely perfect.

A long high whistle caught Sherri's attention. She shoved the brochures back into her purse and peered down the road. A moment later a young man appeared whistling a tune. He was impeccably dressed in tan slacks and a crisp white shirt. He looked so clean-cut and polished that he reminded Sherri of those young men who used to show up on her parents' doorstep on Saturday mornings holding gilded copies of the Bible. But what stood out most about this man was his blindingly bright, neon-orange vest.

"Excuse me," Sherri called, getting to her feet.

Without missing a beat in his stride, the man started waving. "Hello, hello! Welcome!"

He looked so animated, so happy to see her that for a moment Sherri thought he had been expecting her. Could this be Uncle Walter? No, it couldn't be. Uncle Walter was at least thirty years older. And as the man got close, she saw the nametag pinned to his vest: DOUGLAS, SALES ASSOCIATE.

"Well hello there," the man said, taking her hand in an enthusiastic shake. "My name's Doug. You just get into town?"

Sherri nodded, feeling a bit uneasy. "Uh, hi Doug. I'm Sherri. Yeah, I just got here."

"Staying on a while, I hope."

"For the summer. Hey, I was wondering . . ."

"Are you by any chance looking for work?" he interrupted.

"Excuse me?" Sherri said. "No, I'm not looking for work. I'm looking for the town."

"We're always looking to bring people into the Shopwells family. Hold on a sec." He slid his backpack off his shoulder and rummaged inside.

"Shopwells? The big box store?"

"You've heard of us—wonderful!"

"Sure. Everyone's heard of Shopwells."

Douglas pulled out a clipboard and pen and offered them to Sherri. "Shopwells is so much more than your average big box store. We're a lifestyle solution. Here's a job application in case you change your mind. You'd make a fine member of our Shopwells family."

"You carry that around with you, huh? That's some aggressive recruiting."

The placid smile never left Douglas' face, and Sherri wondered if he was on drugs.

"Listen, I really just wanted to know how far it is to town? I mean, if I had to walk there."

"Not far at all. It's only about a mile down that way." The man pointed in the opposite direction from where the bus had disappeared. "In fact, I'm headed into town to get to work. Come on. I'll show you the way."

"That's pretty far."

"A fit employee is a healthy employee," Douglas said in an even tone that made it sound like he was reciting from a manual. "And a healthy employee is a productive employee. Shopwells cares a great deal about the health of its workers. In fact, we offer a flu shot to all new hires. Tonight I'm working the evening shift. You'd think it would be tiring, but working at Shopwells is exhilarating. Helping the customers is all the reward I need."

"Uh, right. Thanks for the offer, but maybe I'll just wait for my aunt." *Aunt Gillian*, she thought, *you can come any time now, please and thanks and save me from this whack job!*

As if on cue, a wood-panelled station wagon badly in need of a tune-up rattled into the parking lot. Sherri let out a long sigh. "That must be her," she said, grabbing her suitcase.

The station wagon's horn beeped twice, and an arm covered in about a million, jangling silver bracelets darted out the window and waved.

"Sherri? Sherri dear, helloooo!" called a singsong voice as the car stopped.

"Nice to meet you, Douglas," Sherri said over her shoulder as she rushed toward the station wagon.

"See you at Shopwells," he called back. "You'll shop well at Shopwells."

Aunt Gillian climbed out of the car. Her hair was an unnatural, almost violent shade of red twisted up in a bun that had come loose around the base of her neck so that strands flew about her face. Her bright blue eyes sparkled as she beamed at Sherri. She wore a long, flowing peasant skirt and a frilly blouse. When she stepped over to give Sherri a hug, Aunt Gillian's body jiggled along with the frills and ruffles of her clothes. "Welcome, dear. Welcome!"

Sherri couldn't answer. Her face was muffled against her aunt's giant bosom, which smelled like baking spices and beeswax. Sherri returned her hug with enthusiasm.

"Let me take a good look at you," Aunt Gillian said, releasing Sherri and slipping a pair of glasses onto the tip of her nose. "My goodness, you're a woman now! What are you now? Eighteen? Nineteen? Your uncle and I haven't seen you since you were barely walking."

"I'm almost eighteen."

"Let's get your suitcase in the car. You must be exhausted after your trip, and I've got a nice dinner staying warm in the oven for you."

Aunt Gillian put Sherri's suitcase into the trunk and slid into the car. Sherri fastened her seatbelt and glanced over her shoulder. The entire back seat was loaded with cardboard boxes stacked right up to the rear window.

"What's all that stuff?"

"That's why I was late. I was down at Shopwells. They were having the most marvellous sale on canning supplies, and I guess I lost track of time."

"You must be planning to do a lot of canning, huh?"

"Oh, Sherri dear, we're a berry farm as well as a bed and breakfast."

The boxes of jars looked like Aunt Gillian was preparing for an army of guests.

"You just wait until you try my blueberry and raspberry jam," Aunt Gillian said as she shoved an ancient-looking cassette tape into the dashboard. A mournful country tune played softly. "I'll bet you won't want to go back to Toronto in September without a whole case of my delicious jam."

As they rolled away, Sherri glanced out her window at the empty lot. A lone light bulb flickered to life over the welcome sign swaying in the summer breeze.

"Aunt Gillian," Sherri asked, "what's up with the bus stop?"

"Up, dear?" Aunt Gillian asked, half watching the road, half glancing at herself in the rearview mirror. "Oh dear, I am a sight, aren't I? This is no way to greet a new guest."

"I'm not *really* a guest. I'm family."

"Of course, dear. But you're *our* guest. And I feel a little embarrassed because there was a time when you'd never catch me with a hair out of place or without my good pearls on when I came to meet a new batch of guests," she said, sighing.

"I wasn't even sure this was Lewton," Sherri said. "The bus stop looks so rundown. The driver said they might take Lewton off their route. Aren't tourists coming up here anymore?"

"Just a lull, dear. We're just in a little lull," her aunt said. "But Shopwells is turning things around. Since they opened their new flagship store, it's been like night and day. Your Uncle Walter says so."

"Like night and day?"

"Oh, well, because it's . . ." Aunt Gillian furrowed her brow as if she couldn't quite remember why. "It's just been a godsend. That's what Uncle Walter says."

They lapsed into an uncomfortable silence, until Sherri dug the Berry Grove brochure out of her purse.

"Hey, check out what I found in the restaurant where we stopped for lunch."

Aunt Gillian glanced at the brochure. "Well now. They still have those out, do they? How lovely. We had those printed ages ago. When we get home, though, please don't show it to your Uncle Walter. We're a little behind on getting those updated. It will just remind him of one more thing that needs to be done and, really, he's had so much on his mind lately. Look, here we are!"

The station wagon's headlights caught the fading letters of a sign at the edge of the road: BERRY GROVE BED AND BREAKFAST: HOMEMADE JAMS AND JELLIES FOR SALE. A red arrow pointed left.

# CHAPTER TWO

**"HOME, SWEET HOME," AUNT GILLIAN CHIRPED AS THEY PULLED** into the empty lot in front of the house.

Sherri felt a surge of excitement, but that deflated when she caught a glimpse of her new home for the summer. The Berry Grove Bed and Breakfast seemed to sag in the middle, like it was about to cave in on itself and be sucked into the earth. The gleaming white exterior in the brochure had faded to a mottled grey, with large chunks of the paint peeled away entirely. The flower gardens were still there, but they were overgrown and choked with weeds. A porch light illuminated a jagged tear in the screen door, and one of the shutters on a nearby window hung precariously from a single hinge.

"Well, what do you think, dear?" her aunt asked.

"Um, it's great," Sherri finally managed to say.

Aunt Gillian pulled Sherri's bags from the trunk. "Let's get you settled."

Sherri followed her aunt up the front walk, with its heaving cobblestones and upstart weeds. Aunt Gillian hummed a little tune as she led the way across the groaning porch where the swing that Sherri had spotted in the brochure dangled awkwardly from a single chain.

"I've been after your Uncle Walter to set that swing to rights for weeks now," Aunt Gillian said, sounding as if she were talking about a crooked nail or a tilted painting. "But he hasn't been feeling too well lately."

"Oh? What's wrong?" Sherri asked, picking up on the halting tone in her aunt's voice. "Is he sick?"

"We'll get the swing back up for you, don't worry," her aunt said. "It's lovely to sit out here and have a nice swing in the evenings after a hot day. You would think the guests would want to keep to themselves in their rooms. But no, I was forever bringing folks teas and little sweets well into the night because they couldn't bear to leave the porch."

The front door squeaked on its hinges as Aunt Gillian ushered Sherri into the dim kitchen. Sherri stood still for a minute in the darkness while her aunt bustled about, turning on lamps. Aside from the sound of Aunt Gillian's shoes on the floor, Sherri heard no movement in the cavernous house.

"Where's Uncle Walter?"

"He's at work, dear," Aunt Gillian said. "I dropped him off in town before I came to get you. He's sorry he wasn't here to greet you. But you'll be seeing a lot of each other this summer, don't you worry about that."

"At work?" Sherri asked.

"Oh yes, at Shopwells." Aunt Gillian practically sang. Sherri felt her stomach drop.

"Shopwells?" Something about the thought of Uncle Walter stocking shelves or helping customers alongside that weirdo Douglas creeped Sherri out. "But I thought you said he's sick. Is he well enough to be at work?"

"Oh, no, dear. It's not as bad as all that . . . your uncle's just not quite himself. Now, if you'll just give me a moment, I simply *must* get the heat back on under this batch of plum raspberry." As Aunt Gillian fired up the stove under a massive cauldron, Sherri gazed around, taking everything in.

An old spinning wheel coated with dust sat tucked in the corner of the kitchen, and a bricked hearth and fireplace decorated with cast iron pots took up the entire far wall. Hooked rugs with clashing South American-style patterns covered the wooden floor at odd angles. Everything seemed a mishmash. Sherri's eyes darted from watercolours to dangling marionettes to a dusty curio cabinet crammed with cut crystal on one shelf and collectible glasses from a fast food chain on the next. It looked like someone had started decorating one part of the room and then, by the time they'd moved on to the next part, had forgotten their original scheme and started all over again.

Tourist magazines and flyers covered a long counter that separated the dining space from the cooking area. A large oval-shaped table in the centre of the dining room was set with white dishes patterned with blue flowers. Ten place settings were meticulously laid out, complete with folded blue napkins under the cutlery. But a fine layer of dust coated the cups, saucers and plates. Even the bouquet of silk flowers arranged in a blue vase at the centre of the table looked faded and worn.

At the head of the table, one square was highly polished with a place setting ready for Sherri. "Sit, dear. I hope you like meatloaf, string beans and mashed potatoes," Aunt Gillian said, placing the food down.

"Are you expecting more guests tonight, Aunt Gillian?" Sherri asked, slipping into her seat.

"Oh, that," Aunt Gillian said, wiping her hands on a dishtowel. "I like to keep the place prepared. Even if we don't have anyone down in the book, you never know when someone will show up. Here, I'll show you." Aunt Gillian brought Sherri a thick volume bound in creased leather that had been resting on a side table near the front door. She flipped to a page marked with a fraying red ribbon. "You see? These are all the people who've stayed with us at one time or another." She turned the pages. Scribbled names, dates and addresses filled all of them. Sherri glanced at the cities: Toronto, Montreal, Ottawa, Sudbury, Buffalo.

"Wow—Miami," Sherri said. But when she flipped the pages forward, she saw that the most recent guest signature was dated almost a year before: *Rebecca Scott, Niagara Falls, Ontario. June 15, 2009.* Aunt Gillian tapped her finger on the name.

"She was the student reporter last summer."

"I didn't know the person who had the job last year stayed here," Sherri said. "What was she like? Did she like the job?"

"Oh yes. Rebecca even stayed on to work at the paper full time. She's a very nice girl. Quiet, very serious. She had just graduated from university. They used to get university students for that summer position."

"They did?" Sherri asked. "This year they advertised for a high school senior. Why would they do that if it's always been university students before?"

"Oh, who's to say, dear?" Aunt Gillian shrugged. "I'm sure when they took a look at *your* work they thought: 'Why, here's someone who will easily run circles around all those university students!'"

Sherri gave a half-smile. Why would the newspaper switch from university students to high school kids?

"Did Rebecca get along with the boss?" she asked. "Did she say anything about the editor, Mr. MacLachlan? I only spoke to him on the phone once. He seemed all right."

"Oh, Mac's a lamb," Aunt Gillian said as she closed the guest book and returned to her bubbling pot of jam on the stove.

Sherri hoped that was true. When Mr. MacLachlan had called her two weeks before to tell her she had gotten the student reporter job, he had sounded harried and distracted, like he was doing a dozen things at once. "Your level of experience looks perfect, Miss . . . uh, Richmond. Just what, uh, just what we need." Sherri had only half heard him—she'd been dancing a victory dance around her tiny bedroom. But now Mr. MacLachlan's exact words, that sense of hesitation in his voice when he said, "Your level of experience looks perfect," came back to her.

What had he meant by *that*?

"Come over here, dear," Aunt Gillian called, now that Sherri had finished her dinner. "I want to show you something that I'm rather proud of." Behind the counter, past the stove, towered a massive oak pantry. Aunt Gillian flung the doors open to reveal what looked to be about a billion jars of jam.

"Um . . . that's . . ." For once, Sherri found herself at a loss for something to say.

"Impressive, isn't it?"

"Sure. Yes, we'll go with that. It's certainly a lot of jam." Sherri peered at row after row of labels neatly handwritten in blue ink.

"Blueberry, raspberry, cherry. Almond and red pepper?" she asked, wrinkling her nose in distaste before she could stop herself.

"I'm always trying out new things," Aunt Gillian said, straightening out a couple of errant jars so that they stood at perfect right angles.

"But what about all those jars still in the car?"

"Dear?" Aunt Gillian said, as if she didn't understand the question. "What about them?"

*What about them! Unless you've been commissioned by the military to be the sole provider of jam for the troops, I'm thinking you may have enough for now.*

For a moment Aunt Gillian looked as if she understood. But she didn't. "Oh, of course, what a treasure you are. We should bring those jars in. Would you mind, dear? Keys to the car are up front."

**A** few minutes later, Sherri tottered in with the first box.

"Wonderful, just place it over in the nook with the others, dear," Aunt Gillian said, pointing to a dark alcove behind the jam pantry.

*Others?* At the entrance to the alcove, she clicked on the light and nearly dropped the box of jars. "What *is* all this?"

The small room was crammed from floor to ceiling with teetering piles of appliances, most in their original boxes still plastered with neon orange stickers that read: *Thank you for shopping well at Shopwells.*

"Those are just my things," Aunt Gillian said. "You wouldn't believe the sales that they have. Why, combined with your uncle's employee discount, I mean, I'd be losing money if I didn't buy these things! And they have the niftiest gadgets. Did you know that there's such a thing as an electric potato peeler? Oh, I know what you're thinking, but it works wonderfully on carrots as well."

Sherri laughed, but stopped when Aunt Gillian didn't join in. "Why is it all stuffed back here?"

"I've been too busy making jam and haven't had time to sort it all."

Sherri wanted to ask if that wonderful store ever had sales on house paint or on repair kits to fix that dangling swing outside. "But do you really need a . . . a . . . what on earth *is* this?" she asked, holding up a dusty box.

"That? Why that's a coffee maker, dear," Aunt Gillian said.

"But you have a coffee maker right there on your counter."

"Oh, but *this* coffee maker plays music when the brewing is done. Why, just look! You can program it to play your favourite artist. Imagine hearing Conway Twitty croon to let me know my cuppa is ready? It's charming! I'm not quite sure how to make it *work* yet. The instructions are a bit confusing. But don't worry. I promise you will hear Conway Twitty over a cup of coffee before your stay with us is over."

"Hoo boy," Sherri muttered, and closed the door on the mountain of ridiculous appliances. Sherri wondered what Uncle Walter thought about the lifetime supply of pepper almond jam and the closet full of singing appliances. This kitchen reminded her of those TV shows about hoarders.

"So when is Uncle Walter coming home?" She peered around a corner into the dusty living room. "I'd like to say hi."

*And ask him just what the heck is going on here,* she thought.

"He doesn't get off until midnight. And you'll want to be in bed early so you can be bright-eyed and bushy-tailed for your first day at the newspaper."

# CHAPTER THREE

AUNT GILLIAN TOOK SHERRI TO HER ROOM. THE BERRY GROVE farmhouse was a labyrinth of narrow corridors and staircases that appeared out of nowhere and disappeared into darkness. Lugging her suitcase up one flight of stairs after another, Sherri couldn't help but wonder if she should be leaving a trail of breadcrumbs so that she could find her way out again.

*No, not breadcrumbs: pebbles,* Sherri thought. *It has to be pebbles. The birds ate the breadcrumbs.*

"We have six guest rooms up here," Aunt Gillian said, tapping each door as they passed. "I'm afraid I spent so much time getting yours ready that I've neglected the others a smidge. But I'll show them to you after I've dusted. Up there is your room, dear."

Sherri gazed up another dark narrow staircase. "In the attic?"

"Best room in the house. It has a private bath. We call it the lavender room, and it's all yours—unless another guest comes to join us. We've had guests fight over that room."

Sherri pictured a bare mattress on the floor, tucked in between piles of old TV guides or jars of jam. But at the top of the groaning staircase, she smelled fresh lavender even before

Aunt Gillian nudged the door open. Inside, a four-poster bed with a flower-printed comforter dominated one wall. Against another, there was a chest of drawers and a floor-length mirror. They looked like antiques, if a bit bedraggled. Lace curtains covered the large windows, and the room had a lovely cozy country feel to it.

A flood of relief welled up in Sherri as she looked around the room and got a sense of what the Berry Grove Bed and Breakfast must have been like in its glory days. "It's just wonderful," she said.

"Why don't you make yourself comfortable, and I'll call your mother to let her know you've arrived safely."

"Thanks," Sherri said. "Oh hey, you wouldn't happen to have a copy of *Jane Eyre*? I left mine on the bus."

Aunt Gillian frowned. "I don't think I've heard of it, dear. But you can help yourself to anything that's on my bookshelf. I have a splendid collection."

Sherri smiled politely. "No, I'd really like to finish mine first. I read it every summer, and I'm just at the part where Jane Eyre discovers the lunatic in the attic."

"That sounds too dark for my tastes, dear. I just finished *The Cowboy Wants a Wife*. It wasn't quite as good as *The Bride Wore Boots*, but I certainly enjoyed it. I'm sure you can find a copy of *Jane's Heirs* at Anita's Bookshop. It's the only one in town. It's on Main Street. Try her tomorrow."


After unpacking her suitcase, Sherri flipped open her cellphone and felt relieved to see she had a signal. She dialled Michael, hoping he would be in a better mood than he had been the night before she left. Their goodbye evening had crashed and burned, and he hadn't even shown up at the bus station to see her off. Sherri was worried that he was still angry with her.

"Hey, it's Mike. Tell me what's up."

Was he deliberately not answering? Sherri didn't leave a message. Instead she tapped out a text. *I miss you. Call me back.*

Yawning, Sherri placed her cellphone on the nightstand and climbed onto bed fully dressed. She was tired, but she wanted to stay awake a little longer in case Michael called.

Sherri sat bolt upright in the pitch-black room. It took her a split second to realize that she wasn't alone. Someone else was in the room, someone standing close. Her eyes adjusted to the darkness just enough to make out the shape of a dark figure coming toward her. Cold dry fingers circled her wrist, squeezing, and Sherri screamed, yanking herself backward and toppling off the bed.

"Help!" she screamed, scrambling for the light switch.

"What on earth is going on?" a frantic voice called out.

The overhead light suddenly blazed.

Aunt Gillian was standing in the doorway, one hand poised over the switch, the other gripping her chest as if she was about to have a coronary.

"You fell asleep in your clothes, dear!" Her face, pale, lined and stripped of makeup, was twisted.

Between her and Sherri stood a white-haired man in striped blue pajamas and bare feet. He gripped a Styrofoam takeout food container, and his belly hung out over the waistband of his pajama bottoms. He looked confused.

"Uncle Walter?" Sherri gasped. "What are you doing?"

"You . . ." Uncle Walter said with great effort, licking his lips. "You should try the staff special." He held out the container to her. "Let me know if you need help finding anything. At Shopwells, we're here to help."

"Aunt Gillian?"

Her aunt glided forward and placed a gentle hand on Uncle Walter's forearm. "Walter, honey, you're not at work, you're at home, dear. And this is Sherri, your niece. She's come to stay with us, remember?"

Uncle Walter gave his head a shake, then turned from Sherri to Aunt Gillian. "I'm sorry I . . . Was I doing it again, Jilly?"

"It's all right, dear," she said, guiding him back toward the door. "You head on back to bed. No harm done."

*No harm done!* Sherri wanted to shout. *How about me being half-dead of a heart attack? I think that would qualify as some serious harm.*

"Aunt Gillian," Sherri said in a sharp whisper. "What the hell was *that*?"

"Shh!" Aunt Gillian jabbed an index finger up to her lips. "He's half asleep, dear. You mustn't jolt him out of it. It's not good for him."

"He was sleepwalking?"

"I'm so sorry," Aunt Gillian said, glancing down the stairway as Uncle Walter disappeared onto the landing below. "I should have told you. Since he got that job at Shopwells he's been doing this. They're working him too hard. You should get out of your street clothes and go back to bed. It'll be morning soon."

Sherri sat awake in the darkness for a long time. She was rattled, half expecting to hear Uncle Walter's creaking footsteps on the staircase. But all she heard was the thud thud of her heart pounding in her ears.


The next morning she looked at her phone, hoping to find a text from Michael. There was nothing. *Okay, fine. Screw you.* She tucked the phone into her purse and headed down for breakfast. The twisting turning corridors of the Berry Grove farmhouse didn't seem quite so ominous in the morning light. In the kitchen, everything looked normal and bright, with sunlight streaming through the yellowing lace curtains and Aunt Gillian standing over the stove, cracking eggs into a sizzling skillet.

"Hey," Sherri said, slipping into the room.

"Good morning! Don't you look professional for your first day!"

Sherri wore the best first-day-of-work outfit she could think of: black slacks, a neat white blouse and a green vest. "Thanks," she said, glancing around for Uncle Walter. But it was just the two of them in the kitchen.

"I hope you were able to get back to sleep," Aunt Gillian said, looking away.

"Oh . . . sure. No problem," Sherri lied as she slipped into a chair. "Is Uncle Walter joining us?" she asked, trying to sound casual.

"He never eats my cooking anymore. He's just nuts about the food they serve for staff at Shopwells. If I weren't a good cook I might be jealous." Aunt Gillian gave a little laugh, but her voice had an edge to it. She approached Sherri with the coffee pot, and Sherri felt grateful that it didn't croon a Conway Twitty tune.

"Is there orange juice?"

"In the fridge, second shelf from the top," Aunt Gillian said, returning to the stove. "Help yourself."

Sherri got up and went over to the giant old-fashioned fridge. It was packed and ready to feed a full house. But as she reached for the carton of juice, her eyes froze on a Styrofoam container. It was the same one Uncle Walter had clutched last night in her room. She lifted the lid and peaked inside. It was a congealed mess of something like shepherd's pie, with greyish, fatty granules of meat, mushy looking peas and limp kernels of corn.

"Well look who's up," Uncle Walter called as he entered the kitchen.

Sherri slammed the fridge so suddenly that the empty jam jars on top rattled. "Uh, hi, Uncle Walter."

He looked nothing like the dead-eyed sleepwalker from the night before. His blue eyes sparkled, his hair was combed back and his white beard and moustache looked perfectly trimmed. His tidy slacks had been ironed to perfection, and his white shirt shone in the sunshine streaming in from the open door.

"So sorry I wasn't here to welcome you when you arrived," he said. "But your aunt tells me that you're all settled in. Did you get a good night's sleep?"

Aunt Gillian shot Sherri a pleading look, shook her head and mouthed the word *no*. But Sherri ignored her. "I had a bit of trouble sleeping last night."

Oblivious, Uncle Walter chuckled as he filled a mug with black coffee. "Bet you're not used to the quiet out here," he said. "But watch, by the time you head back to the city you're going to be so used to the country you'll need a set of earplugs over there."

"Breakfast is ready!" Aunt Gillian said a bit too cheerily as she scooped fluffy scrambled eggs onto a plate for Sherri.

Uncle Walter moved to the fridge, pulled out his Styrofoam container and dug a fork in without even heating up the food. There was something about his smile that unnerved Sherri. She realized with a shiver that it was the same kind of smile that never left that guy Douglas' face at the bus stop. Cool, placid and vacant.

"Aunt Gillian said you work at Shopwells. What do you do there?"

"Wonderful place to work. I'm in the automotive department. We've got a great deal on synthetic motor oil right now. You oughta stop by and check it out."

"Sherri, you need to eat up," Aunt Gillian interrupted, her voice stern. "I'm not sending you to your first day of work on an empty stomach."

"Would you like to try some of this?" Uncle Walter asked, holding the Styrofoam container out to her. "This will fill you up."

"Walter," Aunt Gillian cautioned. "Will you let the child finish what I've made for her?"

"That's all right, Aunt Gillian," Sherri said, scooping the last of the eggs off her plate. "I'm all done and I'm *really* full. Great breakfast!"

"How about I show you around a bit?" Uncle Walter said.

"Must've been close to dark when you got in yesterday. I'll take you out to the fields and show you where the magic happens."

"Now, Walter," Aunt Gillian said deliberately. "You know Sherri has to be off to her big new job. It's her first day, remember?"

Confusion flashed across Uncle Walter's face, and Sherri glimpsed the same dazed slack expression that he had during the night. Aunt Gillian reached over and gave Uncle Walter's hand a squeeze. He shook his head, as if brushing the confusion away. His smile returned.

"Of course. Well maybe a tour of the berry fields on the weekend then? Or maybe when you're back from work? It's your first day. Mac won't keep you in the office too late."

"What's he like?" Sherri asked.

"Originally from the city, like you. He's nice enough. A bit frazzled. A bit intense. You'll like him."

"Well, I should hit the road. I want to be a bit early on my first day. Mom said you might lend me the car. Is that okay? Mr. MacLachlan said I'd need a car for assignments."

"Well," Aunt Gillian said, "that's something we wanted to talk to you about . . ."

*Uh oh,* Sherri thought. *They've changed their minds. But I can't be a reporter on foot or, God forbid, a bicycle. How would that look? Racing to the scene of a bank robbery or a house fire on a ten-speed?*

"Your uncle and I had a talk about how to arrange the driving while you're here with us. Go on out to the garage. He's got something to show you."

"Um, okay."

The grass glittered with dew, and a flock of black-capped chickadees tittered from the branches of the giant old willow tree. Uncle Walter threw open the barn-style garage doors with a flourish. Sherri had to squint into the shadows for a moment before she could see the car. It looked old, but not *falling apart* old. Vintage. It took her a second to realize what was happening.

"Is that a Mini? An original Mini Cooper?"

"Used to be our little tool-around car. I've been meaning to get her back up and running again for ages. This seemed like as good a reason as any. She's all yours during your stay."

"Are you serious?" Sherri asked, gaping. "You're lending me my very own car? Thank you, Uncle Walter!" She threw her arms around his neck and kissed his papery cheek. Uncle Walter pulled away, looking embarassed.

"Your aunt and I just use the station wagon now. Seemed a shame to let Betsey here go to waste when she might get a few more miles on her this summer."

"Betsey?"

"That's her name. Your aunt always said it was a good name for a cute little thing."

"I'll take good care of her. I promise."


As she drove down the long driveway, Sherri honked and waved out the window.

# CHAPTER FOUR

**AS SHE CRUISED TOWARD WORK, SHERRI FIDDLED WITH THE OLD**
radio in the Mini. All she could tune in through the static was
a garbled snippet from a local gospel station.

"Covetousness is an illness! It is the insatiable thirst for
riches when you are already filled with them . . ."

She turned the dial and finally caught a chirpy tune sung
by a chorus of women in a doo-wop style.

> *Everyone around is sure to tell you,*
> *Whether you want milk or chairs or glue,*
> *Everything you need for home and office*
> *At Shopwells it's all waiting here for you.*

Sherri flicked off the radio. *Milk, chairs and glue?*

As she rolled up to the stop sign at the end of the road, the
car began to shake. The brake pedal vibrated under her foot.

"Oh no. C'mon, Betsey, what's wrong? Don't do something
hasty on my first day, girl."

Betsey lurched and sputtered, and then her engine died.
Sherri sank against the steering wheel, sighing. She reached
for her cell. No signal, so she got out to take a look under

the hood. *Wouldn't Michael think this is hysterical—me trying to make sense of a car's engine.* That thought reminded her that Michael still hadn't returned her message from the night before.

*One crisis at a time,* she thought.

Sherri stepped away from the car and looked up and down the road. She couldn't walk back to the farmhouse; it was too far. Quicker to find help close by. Not far ahead, a bright red mailbox was perched on the edge of the road. A driveway leading to a small wood cottage was visible through the trees. Perfect. As if on cue, someone emerged from the front door. Sherri beeped the horn and waved. "Hello!" she called.

The woman waved back half-heartedly, thrust her hands into the pockets of her cargo shorts and walked up to Sherri. She looked about thirty-five years old and wore a faded red sweater and hiking boots. "Morning," the woman said. "Car trouble?"

"Yeah." Sherri gestured helplessly toward the car. "It just kind of lurched and vibrated, then died. I can't get a cell signal out here. Can I use your phone and call my uncle?"

The woman cocked her head at Sherri. "You must be the new reporter, huh?"

"How did you know that?"

"You're in a small town. Everyone knows everything about everyone. I'm Paula."

"Sherri."

"Mind if I take a look?" Before Sherri could answer, Paula ducked under the hood. With a quick twist of her wrist and a tug at a wire, she poked around. "Give it a try now."

Sherri got into the driver's seat and turned the key. The

engine rumbled back to life. "That's great! What did you do?" Sherri asked, leaping back out of the car.

"Just a loose wire," Paula said as she slammed the hood shut. "Should be fine now. So, the new reporter, huh? How did you hear about a job in Lewton? Where have you worked before?"

"Um, I applied online. There was a job posting."

Paula smiled, but there was something condescending in it. "So typical of the way things are going at that paper," she said. "They want to keep something under wraps, so they hire a kid."

Sherri prickled. "Who's trying to keep what under wraps?"

"Shopwells. My record shop is hanging by a thread; they're buying up all the commercial real estate and letting it go to rack and ruin, and the one person who was getting to the bottom of it—your predecessor—is now working for them."

Sherri felt a shiver as the little hairs on the back of her arms prickled—*a story!* She pictured the front page with a blaring headline and her byline.

"Rebecca Scott? Why did she leave the paper?"

"You'll have to ask her," Paula said. She turned and walked back toward her cottage.


As Sherri drove into town, the first thing she noticed was the ice cream parlour. It looked like the one on the brochure, but the striped awning, faded and torn, hung tattered and whipping in the morning breeze. Yellowed newspaper pages covered the plate-glass windows. Driving past a neglected playground, Sherri recognized the same gazebo as in the brochure. The bench inside had collapsed in a heap of worn planks, and beer bottles littered the floor.

*I could get a splinter just by looking at it.*

Sherri felt more and more alarmed as she glanced from empty storefront to empty storefront. Sidewalk planters were overgrown with weeds. She drove through what looked like the town's lone traffic light and pulled up next to a rusty parking meter in front of a big yellow house. An old-fashioned wooden sign on the lawn read: THE LEWTON LEADER-POST. The house was immaculate, with freshly painted shutters and gleaming windows. Sherri shoved a quarter into the meter, but it just kept flashing zeros.

*I'd better not get a ticket on my first day!*

A little bell clanged overhead as Sherri stepped inside the office.

An older woman with frizzy orange hair looked up from behind a giant oak desk. "Can I help you?"

"I'm the new reporter." She jerked her thumb back toward the street. "I'm not going to get a ticket, am I?"

The woman laughed. "Jim hasn't been replaced since he started working at Shopwells. So you're safe. I'm Vivienne, but everyone around here just calls me Viv." Viv reached across the desk and pumped Sherri's hand.

Sherri felt the tips of the woman's acrylic fingernails scrape against her palm. It sent a shudder up her spine, but she kept smiling.

"Welcome," Viv continued. "It's so nice to have a fresh face—and all the way from Toronto! How exciting."

"Thanks," Sherri said. "I'm excited to get started." She glanced around the front office foyer. Framed Group of

Seven reproductions hung on the wood-panelled walls. Faded editions of *Cottage Life* and the newspaper itself littered the coffee table in the waiting area.

"Go right up," Viv said, pointing the way with the stub of a pencil. "Mac is waiting for you. That's Ted. *Mister* MacLachlan, I suppose. We all just call him Mac. You will too. Just up the stairs. I'll call up to let him know you're coming."

"Thank you," Sherri said, climbing the creaky wooden staircase. The lemony scent of furniture polish tickled her nose.

"Mac?" Sherri heard Viv say. "Sherri Richmond is on her way up." Viv hung up the phone by the time Sherri reached the first landing. Sherri stopped there for a moment. Glancing down at the front desk, all she could see were those polished red nails clacking on the keypad as Viv dialled another number.

"She's here," Viv said just loud enough for Sherri to hear. Now her voice sounded entirely different. "No, it doesn't look like it will be a problem."

At the top of the stairs, Sherri walked up to a door with the word EDITOR stencilled in gold letters on the frosted glass. Sherri half expected to find a Walter Matthau type inside, tugging on his suspenders and sucking a fat cigar. She tapped her knuckles against the glass. "Hello?"

"Come in." The voice was harried.

Inside the small bright office, behind a desk covered with papers and photographs and notepads, sat a slim short man in a black golf shirt. "Just a moment, just finishing this sentence," Mac said, typing furiously with his index fingers— hunting and pecking, Sherri's typing teacher used to call it. Mac looked pale and intent as he stared with determination at his computer screen. Sherri's picture of a pot-bellied, cigar-chomping editor quickly vanished.

Mac's face looked haggard and drawn, like he was in desperate need of a good home-cooked meal. Finally, he swivelled away from the computer. "You must be Sherri Richmond. I'm Mac. Nice to finally meet you in person." He leaned across the desk to greet Sherri with a limp clammy handshake. "Please, have a seat."

"Thanks so much," Sherri said, sitting down. "I have a couple of questions."

Mac laughed. "Champing at the bit, are you? Don't worry, I'll give you the grand tour of the office. To answer your questions: lunch is whenever you have time for it, you get forty-five minutes, tops, and yes, you will have access to Facebook and other social networks. But we do have the capability to block them, so please be sure you use them only for official newspaper business. Also there's . . ."

"No, no," Sherri interrupted. "Sorry, I mean that's all great. But I actually had a couple of questions about Rebecca."

Mac's eyes widened and he stiffened in his seat. "What did you want to know about her?"

"I heard that she's working at Shopwells now. Is that true?"

Mac's smile thinned into a straight line. "It is."

"So she quit her job?"

"Well, they offered her more money. I liked her. She was a good reporter. Who told you about her leaving the newspaper?"

Sherri hesitated. "Just someone I ran into."

"Protecting your sources?" Mac said with a smile.

"Not at all. It was a woman I ran into this morning on my way in. Her name was Paula."

Mac laughed. "You'll learn, Richmond. In this business, news is only as worthwhile as the source you get it from."

"Why isn't Paula a good source?"

"Well it's like this: every town has its types. In Lewton, we have the nosy churchgoer—that's Penny Potter. You'll meet her soon enough. We have our barfly, John Fisher, and then we have Paula Simcoe—conspiracy theorist."

"What do you mean by that?" Sherri asked, biting her lip.

"She's something of a radical when it comes to Shopwells. She organized protests, even stood in front of the bulldozers." Mac shook his head. "A bit of a wing nut, if you ask me."

"What about all the businesses shutting down?"

"It's called progress," Mac said.

"Well, I'd like to look into it."

"Shopwells and everything that goes on with Town Hall are Krystal's beat. She's the municipal reporter. Took over for Rebecca. You're the community reporter, okay. Now that we've got that all sorted out, why don't I give you the ten-cent tour, huh? Show you where you'll be hunkered down for the summer."

"Sure."

Sherri followed Mac out into the creaking central hallway. Of the four doors leading onto the hall, all but one were closed.

"Aren't many people here right now," Mac said. "Actually, even when everyone *is* here there aren't a lot of people here. In fact, it's just you, me, Krystal, Bill and Viv. Bill works over there." Mac nudged his chin toward the door farthest down the hall. "Bill covers the local sports teams, but he also works as a teacher over at Lewton High. A perfect fit, really. But you won't see much of him on account of his day job."

Mac pointed out the supply closet where Sherri could find pens and notebooks, and an office no bigger than a closet where the copy editor came in once a week to look over the pages before the paper went to print.

"And what about this room?" Sherri asked, trying the door handle.

"That's the morgue," Mac said, easing his way between Sherri and the locked door. "It's a bit of a mess right now."

"Why is it locked?"

"We had a problem with people sneaking in and helping themselves to old editions. Everyone wants an extra copy of the article about their kid winning the elementary school spelling bee or catching the biggest bass at the summer fishing derby. Had to put a stop to it before we got cleaned out. Viv keeps the key down at her desk in case we need to have a look at any of the old stuff."

"Isn't everything backed up on computers?"

"Maybe some of the newer editions. Now Krystal, her office is right over here," Mac said, steering Sherri across the hall. "She used to be on the community beat for ages, so if you have any questions, she's your gal. Oh, where was I with the office particulars? Oh, right: we don't really have a dress code around here. What you've got on works. You might want to try runners though. And jeans are just fine. Be ready for anything, that's our motto. In the morning you could be snapping pictures of a ladies' community tea and in the afternoon interviewing the police about a bank robbery."

Sherri's eyes widened. "You guys have bank robberies?"

"Well no," Mac said, scratching his sandy hair. "But we *could*. That's the point, Richmond. Be ready for anything.

Now this," he said, stepping toward the only open door, "will be your office."

Inside the bright bare room sat a desk identical to the one buried in Mac's office. The tall rectangular window faced out onto Main Street. Sherri hadn't expected her own office. She had an urge to call Michael and share her excitement. But then she remembered she was still ticked at him.

"This used to be Krystal's office. But she switched to the bigger one, so you get her old spot."

"It's great," Sherri said, stepping toward the window to peer through the shades into the street below. "Thanks."

"It's a little empty now, but you can help yourself to what you need from the storage closet to get yourself going. If you can't find something there, just give a list of whatever supplies you need to Viv downstairs and she'll order them up for you." Mac led the way back into his office and sat down. "Now, Richmond, here's your first assignment. I need you to scoot over to the Lewton Farmers' Market and grab some colourful shots. We'll pick a photo for the community page. The market sets up every Wednesday in the west side parking lot of the hardware store, but we haven't featured them in a while. The paper comes out every Friday, so your drop-dead deadline is always Thursday at one. But you're better off writing the stories as they come. You don't want to get bogged down."

Mac reached down into a deep drawer in his desk and pulled out a bulky black camera. "Have you ever worked with one of these?"

It looked huge to Sherri, who was used to snapping pictures with her cellphone or, if she was taking shots for the school paper, with a little blue digital camera that Michael had given her for Christmas. "Oh, sure," Sherri lied.

"You'll want to take some time to get comfortable with that," Mac said. "It's an older model, but it does the job. Learn all the various settings. Sometimes you're going to be shooting in places with practically no light at all. The Riverton Arena, where the elementary school kids play peewee hockey, for example. You'll have a hell of a time in there on weekend shoots when Bill's off. We always do. Horrible overhead lighting."

"Peewee hockey?" Sherri asked.

"It's even worse when you have to cover lacrosse," Mac said. "They take out the ice from the arena and leave these grey floors for the kids to play on. That surface sucks up all the light." He shook his head as if it were a major tragedy. "You'll want to take a separate flash whenever you have an assignment there." Mac smiled. "But you'll learn, Richmond. You'll learn."

"Okay," Sherri said. "So what's the angle with the farmers' market story, then?"

Mac shrugged. "That *is* the angle, Richmond. It's Wednesday. The farmers' market is on. This is the community news beat. No undercover investigation. No breaking news. Community news is getting out to all the meetings and events, asking a few questions and snapping some photos. Gotta keep everyone in town happy—give 'em their fifteen minutes. You'll only need enough information for a cutline to run under the photo. No need for an actual story."

"Oh," Sherri said, feeling a twinge of disappointment. "But there *will* be actual stories for the community pages, right? It's not all just photos and cutlines?"

"You want stories? No problem. You can cover the weekly rummage sale at St. Mary's Church when you finish with the market. Penny Potter phoned me about it yesterday. They've been raising money to re-cover the hymnals with imitation leather. You should be able to get three hundred words out of it."

Sherri laughed and waited for Mac to say he was only joking. But Mac just looked at her, serious, and Sherri's laugh died away. "Oh," she said. "Right. Hymnals. Big stuff."

"Be sure to get to St. Mary's bang on at ten. That's when they open. I'll write out the directions for you," Mac said, and he scribbled on the first page of a blank notebook, which he handed to Sherri along with the pen.

"Here are your tools, Richmond. Go get 'em."

# CHAPTER FIVE

*A PHOTO OF A FARMERS' MARKET,* SHERRI THOUGHT AS SHE climbed into Betsey. *Okay, fine. I can start off slow. He's easing me in.* Sherri flipped her notebook open to the page where Mac had written the directions and burst out laughing.

> Drive west on Main Street. Stop at the
> hardware store. You're there.
> St. Mary's is right across the street.

As Sherri steered into the bumpy cracked parking lot, only four lonely display stands were set up. They were next to the entrance of the empty hardware store. Pulling into a spot, she killed the engine and peered out the open window. Except for Betsey, the parking lot was empty. No customers. This was nothing like the bustling Thursday summer market at City Hall, where you had to elbow your way through crowds to get to the peppers and basil, and the air crackled with energy. This place just looked sad.

Behind one stand, a lanky man in a baseball cap and jean overalls leaned back in a folding beach chair while reading a rumpled newspaper. At another, a woman in a straw sun hat watered potted herbs. At the third, Aunt Gillian sat behind a towering display of jam jars. She stood and waved at Sherri. The only other person in sight was a slump-shouldered boy walking through the parking lot. He stopped and looked at Sherri as she slung the camera around her neck and set up for a test shot.

Green eyes. She had only glanced for a second, but could see he was no more than twenty and had big green eyes and reddish-brown hair. Casually, she glanced up again. He stood still, looking back at her and smiling. Sherri smiled back and shot a photo.

"Hey," he called. "Did you clear that with my agent? I don't model for free, you know."

Sherri laughed as the boy walked over.

"Hi. I'm Ben," he said. "I'm going to take a wild stab in the dark and guess that you must be working for the paper, right?"

"Gee, what gave it away?" she asked, holding up her notebook and pen. "Or was it the big camera?"

"I happen to be unusually gifted in the art of perception."

"You here for the farmers' market?"

"Just headed to work at Tony's Luncheonette. You know it?"

"Yoo hoo, Sherri!" Aunt Gillian called, waving.

"Just a sec!" Sherri called back. Then her cell rang. She glanced down at the number and felt her heart drop. *Michael.* "Hang on," she said, looking at Ben. "I've got to take this real quick." She stepped away, and before Michael could speak, said, "Sorry, I can't talk right now."

"What?"

"I'm busy. I'll call you back."

"Let me guess," Michael said. "You're on a story and you can't talk."

"Right. I'll call you from the office later, okay? Bye." She turned back to Ben. "Sorry about that."

"Drop by Tony's for lunch," Ben said. "I'll give you the scoop on this bustling little metropolis of ours."

"I will. Definitely."

Ben loped away and Sherri watched him for a moment before walking over to Aunt Gillian's booth.

"Well isn't this a nice surprise!" Aunt Gillian stepped out to give Sherri a hug. "Are you go___ to take my picture, dear?"

"Sure," Sherri said. "How l___ ___elling your jams here?"

"Just for the last little ___ ___fing up her hair for the photo. "It u___ ___space to sell here. But a space opene___ ___be a nice change of pace until things ___rove."

"How are sales?" Sherri as___ ___ing around the empty lot.

"It's early yet, dear. But I'm sure I won't go home with a single jar."

Sherri snapped a series of photos of her aunt beaming behind a stack of blueberry jam, before she moved on to the next stand. It was dotted with only a handful of potted plants and herbs.

*This,* Sherri thought, *is a picture that tells a story.*

"Hi there," Sherri said to the middle-aged woman

behind the stand. "Lovely plants. Mind if I snap some shots for *The Post*?"

The woman looked up from her dog-eared romance novel and gave Sherri a warm smile. "Sure thing. I can use all the publicity I can get. I'm Marjorie."

"Great," Sherri said, writing down the details. She glanced over to the side of the hardware store and noticed three abandoned stands, along with a few forgotten shopping carts, each with broken handles and missing wheels.

"Looks like some of the vendors are out sick today," Sherri said, placing a potted herb in Marjorie's hands for the photo.

"Yeah, we're disappearing. Just like everything else around here."

"Hold that pose." Sherri snapped half a dozen photos, and then looked out from around the camera. "Why don't you tell me more about that? I've got a few minutes before I have to be at my next assignment."


Sherri sat behind her desk at the computer. Mac leaned over her shoulder, scanning the photos from the St. Mary's rummage sale.

"Nice," Mac said, nodding at her work. "You have a good eye, Richmond."

"Some people say I have two."

Mac smiled at her. "How did that sense of humour go over with Penny Potter and her church ladies?"

"Not well, actually. Nothing really went well with those ladies. Penny Potter was ticked at me for being all of five minutes late."

"Don't say I didn't warn you," Mac said, chuckling.

The rummage sale had reminded Sherri of the farmers' market in more ways than one: a spartan event with no one on hand except a trio of white-haired ladies. The *sale* consisted of little more than two card tables covered with matted stuffed animals, half-dressed Barbie dolls, tarnished cutlery and musty-smelling clothes.

Mac looked at the photos of Penny Potter and the two other ladies, Ida and Mabel, holding a faded wool sweater with a giant red maple leaf emblazoned across it. "This one's good, but not ideal. See the shadow on Penny Potter's face here?" He pointed to a spot on the screen.

"It was kind of hard to avoid shadows, what with the black cloud of death that followed Penny Potter around," Sherri muttered.

"Now, now, Richmond. These are our subscribers. We have to be kind. Touch it up in Photoshop. Now, show me the farmers' market shots."

"Sure," Sherri said, closing the file with the rummage sale pictures. "Actually, Mac, I know you said you only need a cutline for the farmers' market photo, but I can give you a story."

"Found something, did you?"

"I did an interview with Marjorie. It would make a nice piece on the market." She held her breath.

"Sure. Write it up and I'll look it over. Just keep it under two hundred words or Penny Potter will give me hell for not giving *her* a story too. Now, let's see the rest of the pictures."

Sherri clicked on the file and she opened the first picture. It was a shot of Ben. Sherri blushed.

"I see you met Benjamin."

"It was a test shot to check the light settings."

"Quite the jack of all trades, that kid."

Sherri clicked through the rest of the photos.

"I suppose you'd like us to use your aunt's photo on the front page?" Mac joked.

"Actually, we should go with the shot of Marjorie," Sherri said. "She was the one I interviewed for the story."

"Not much action at her booth, was there?" Mac said, frowning. "Have you got another shot with more people? We want the photos in the community section to look lively."

"There *weren't* any people."

"It's about making the most with what you have. You could have pulled Ben in for a photo. Or got all the vendors together for a group shot."

"I didn't know we were supposed to *stage* photos," Sherri said, trying to keep her voice light.

"It's not *staging*, Richmond. I'd send you right back there to reshoot, if I weren't so positive that they've all packed up and gone by now. Just clean up the shot of Marjorie and get me the story on the rummage sale right away."


Sherri flipped open her notebook to the page on Marjorie and started typing up the story. She was on the second paragraph when somebody knocked on her door.

"Well hello there. You must be the new intern."

Sherri looked up to see a woman standing in the doorway, her arms crossed over her chest as if to say: *show me what you've got*. But the woman looked almost as old as the elderly women at the rummage sale. Her hair had been dyed a stark boot-polish black. Her oversized sweatshirt featured a drawing of a kitten with big yellow eyes that made Sherri think of the gross novelty shirts you find at airport gift shops. The woman peered at Sherri over the top of giant glasses with thick black plastic rims that hid half her face.

"Hi there," Sherri said, giving her warmest smile. "You must be Krystal."

"Yes, dear," the woman said, crossing the length of the room in one stride. When Sherri moved to get up, Krystal held up a hand. "Don't get up. I see I'm interrupting you."

"Don't worry. I'm almost finished."

"So Mac's put you right to work then, has he? Oh, let me guess: St. Mary's for the rummage sale."

"You got it."

"Aren't those ladies at St. Mary's just darling? So devoted to the cause."

"So how long did you cover this beat for?"

"Twelve years," Krystal said, beaming.

"Wow," Sherri said. "That's . . . impressive. How did you do this for twelve years without going out of your mind?"

Krystal let out a little laugh that had zero mirth in it. "I sure hope your sense of humour will lighten up our story meetings."

"Right. Well, nice chatting with you, but I'd better get back to work. Mac wants this story right away."

"I'd be happy to help you with it," Krystal said. "I could probably knock it out in five minutes."

"Thanks, but I'm sure you're busy covering the Shopwells real estate story."

Krystal's face darkened. "That's no story."

"Really? That's not what I heard," Sherri countered.

"Then you heard wrong," Krystal said. She reached for Sherri's white digital voice recorder and fidgeted with it. "I've been a reporter since you were in diapers, Sherri. Once you've been around for longer than a day, maybe you'll start to learn the difference between gossip and a real story." Krystal turned and walked out the door.

"Hey!" Sherri called after her. "That's my recorder."

"Oh, silly me," Krystal said, handing it back. "You know, you really should learn shorthand. It's not good to put your faith in gadgets like this." She looked at her watch. "Oops! Better get going. I'm covering the Committee of Adjustment in an hour." Krystal turned and walked out of the office.

"Maybe they'll adjust your attitude, lady," Sherri muttered, turning back to her rummage sale story. But, on a whim, she opened a new file and let her fingers fly:

### FASHION FILE IN LEWTON, ONTARIO
#### BY SHERRI RICHMOND

Today, our prêt-à-porter profile is of one Krystal Grant, a fashion maven from small-town Ontario who reminds us all that a complete lack of taste, a sour face and partial colour-blindness needn't keep anyone off the red carpet, no matter how moth-eaten their clothes may be. In her tent-like kitten sweater and threadbare leggings, Krystal has given us a unique, shabby-chic style. Walk, don't run, to your closest church rummage sale to copy this look, ladies!

Sherri leaned back in her chair and smiled at the little piece. But it wasn't enough to make her feel better about her encounter with Krystal. It was like posting a nasty anonymous message or getting in a good dig at the schoolyard bully.

*No,* Sherri thought, *I have to take some real action.*

"You can grab yourself a late lunch if you like, Richmond," Mac said, trundling by her open door. "Tony's across the street is good."

"Thanks, Mac."

Sherri deleted Krystal's *Fashion File,* then Googled Shopwells' phone number and dialled. A monotone voice answered.

"Thank you for shopping well at Shopwells. How may I help you?"

"Is Rebecca Scott in today?"

# CHAPTER SIX

SHOPWELLS LOOKED LIKE A NORMAL BIG BOX STORE. AFTER THE abandoned ghost-town look of Lewton and the strange encounters with Douglas and Uncle Walter, Sherri had expected something sinister, like a hooded skeleton in a boat ferrying shoppers across a lake of fire, or a three-headed hound of hell guarding the front entrance. But the store itself was nothing but a giant grey box. Normal-looking customers were rushing in pushing empty orange plastic carts. Others were coming out daze-eyed and loaded down with bulging bags of shopping.

*At least now I know where everyone in town is,* Sherri thought, feeling strangely comforted at her first sight of so many townspeople in one place. But her reporter radar went off the moment she stepped through the automatic sliding doors. She had been inside other Shopwells stores before but this one felt different. Or maybe it was Sherri who felt different the moment she stepped inside. It started as a ringing in her ears. At first she thought it was the buzzing of the fluorescent lights. But no, it was something else, a steady droning just underneath the boring muzak being piped in through the sound system. Sherri tried to ignore it, but a headache started to build behind her temples.

"Welcome to Shopwells!" said an elderly woman in a monotone voice.

Sherri nodded to the woman. She was wearing the familiar orange vest.

"We have a red-light special for the next hour only: a twelve-pack of drain opener for only $29.99," the elderly greeter said, pushing a colourful flyer toward Sherri.

"Um, thanks. I'll consider that if I ever have a dozen clogged drains. Can you tell me which way to the . . ." But as Sherri accepted the flyer, the strangest thought crept into her mind. *But what if Aunt Gillian needs that monster pack of drain cleaner? Berry Grove is a huge house with who knows how many bathrooms. Maybe it would be a good thing to have on hand? Wait, what am I doing here?*

She struggled for a moment to clear her thoughts, all the while staring at the flyer and the picture of drain cleaner.

"The drain cleaner is on aisle five," the greeter said.

"No!" Sherri said, snapping out of it. "I mean, no, thank you. But can you tell me where I'd find Rebecca Scott?"

The elderly woman pointed Sherri to the customer service counter, where three women in identical orange vests turned to greet her simultaneously.

"Can we help you?" asked one.

"Well hi there!" said the second.

"What can we do for you?" chirped the third.

"Whoa . . ." Sherri muttered, wondering if this was what Goldilocks felt like when she woke up to find those three bears in her face. "I'm here to see Rebecca Scott?"

"Rebecca Scott, the PR manager? I'd be pleased to help you with that. Is she expecting you?"

"I called earlier. My name's Sherri Richmond."

"Just a moment, please."

While the woman dialled, Sherri gazed at two giant framed photos hanging below the customer service sign. YOUR HOMETOWN TEAM! proclaimed a small banner below the portraits. The first shot was of a chunky man wearing a loud orange tie the same shade as the Shopwells vests. He had red cheeks and a greying crewcut. TOM WILLARD, ASSISTANT MANAGER, the nameplate beneath the photo read. The picture next to him showed a gaunt, pale man in a dark suit wearing tinted glasses that obscured his eyes. His smile looked so unnatural that it seemed closer to a sneer, exposing a glint of white teeth. P.K. PETERSON, STORE MANAGER. As she stared at the two photos, the second customer service clerk slid a flyer over to Sherri.

"While you're waiting, perhaps you'd like to hear about our specials today?"

"Actually," Sherri said, "I already got the scoop on the drain opener." Something tickled in Sherri's head, and she found herself wondering again if she should pick up the special for Aunt Gillian, just in case.

"Oh, but there are wonderful deals in *all* of our departments. Why, just look here! The summer's already upon us and no self-respecting northern woman should start the season without these new hip waders designed especially for her!" The clerk pointed to the flyer. A beaming woman was clad in a hideous pair of waist-high fishing pants emblazoned with pink and purple flowers.

"I'm not really into fishing," Sherri said, but her gaze lingered on the woman. *It does look like she's having fun. And there's even a matching sun hat. They do look sort of cute together. Maybe Uncle Walter likes fishing and we could go together.*

"Excuse me, are you with *The Post*?" the first customer service lady asked.

"Yes."

All three went silent. The woman in front of her suddenly yanked the flyer away.

"Something wrong?" Sherri asked. "I *did* call earlier. I was told Rebecca was here."

"I'm sorry, but we aren't authorized to speak with anyone from the media without express permission from management."

Sherri half-laughed, but the three women looked deadly serious. "You can't speak to the media. But you can talk to me as a customer, right?"

"You're welcome to browse around the sales floor," the first woman said. "Miss Scott will be with you shortly. Next, please!"

Sherri stepped away from the desk to look at a towering display of lake gear: goggles and fins, inner tubes and water wings. A woman stood staring at an inflatable raft while her daughter sat in a shopping cart filled nearly to the top with what looked like giant bags of birdseed.

"You must really like birds," Sherri quipped.

"We have a feeder at home," the woman said absently as she grabbed a second water raft.

"Just one?" Sherri said, eyeing the giant sacks of feed. "You must get, like, Alfred Hitchcock-sized flocks of birds."

The woman just turned and stared, uncomprehending.

"There were a lot of birds in that movie. You know, the one about . . . the birds? Anyway, that's a lot of seed."

"They're on sale," the woman said. "It's a shame to miss out, you know." She tossed two of the swim rafts on top of the birdseed.

"But, Mommy," whined the little girl, "I don't know how to swim!"

"Of course!" the mother said, veering toward the next aisle. "We'll need life jackets too."

It was a madhouse. People crammed the aisles, pushing full buggies. Sherri glanced around and saw the pharmacy and what looked like the women's clothing department, but no sign of where the management offices might be. She glanced up, looking for a sign suspended from the ceiling with directions. But there was only the shiny black sphere that housed the security camera. *Eye in the sky*, Sherri thought, staring at the steady red light.

Sherri began to feel dizzy, as though she were plunging deeper and deeper into a labyrinth. With every turn she was confronted with the smiling face of a Shopwells worker.

"Try our new Shopwells-brand perfume!" *Spray, spray.* Stink of rotting lilacs and patchouli.

"Car air fresheners are on special—they smell like a new car!"

"Shopwells-brand kitty litter is ten percent off."

"How about a new tackle box for your boyfriend? Here, let me get you a shopping cart."

Somehow, Sherri found herself saying yes to all of it. Her cart was loaded down with perfume, car freshener, kitty litter, a tackle box, Draino, a huge tube of SPF 70 sunblock and something that looked like an elaborate pair of scissors but which, on closer inspection, she realized was an ornate candle-wick trimmer with a rhinestone handle.

Sherri dabbed at her forehead with the sleeve of her blouse. The store felt suddenly, oppressively hot. *A cool drink, that's what I need.*

At the cafeteria order counter, Sherri asked for a large Diet Coke.

"We only have Shopwells-brand cola," said the pimply-faced boy at the register.

"Fine, whatever. So long as it's cold."

"Upsize that for just fifty cents more?" said the boy and he held up a giant drink cup that would hold enough cola to slake the thirst of a dehydrated camel.

"Um . . . okay," Sherri heard herself say. Back out in the store, she took a long deep drink and felt her head clear a little. *There, that helped.* As she took another gulp, Sherri noticed the long line of employees at a row of tables in the far corner of the cafeteria. It was blocked off with a white picket fence marked with a sign that read: STAFF ONLY. The workers stared into their plates. Chewed. Spooned more food into their mouths. Chewed and swallowed. They were eating in unison.

"Sherri?" a smooth pleasant voice called.

Sherri turned and saw a young woman gliding toward her.

"I'm Rebecca Scott." She had a giant perfect smile plastered on her face. She clasped Sherri's outstretched hand in both of hers. "What a nice surprise to get a call from you! How are things at *The Post*? Are you enjoying it?"

"I am, thanks."

Rebecca wore a dark tailored suit, plain black pumps and a white blouse buttoned right up to the neck. Her hair was pulled back into a tight bun. "I see you were checking out our new cafeteria," Rebecca said. "We just opened it to the public. Previously we only had a cafeteria for our workers. But Shopwells thought it was important to give shoppers the full retail experience, including a stop for lunch."

"It looks like everyone's really enjoying the food. I know my uncle's kind of addicted to the staff special. It's like a shepherd's pie, right?"

"And who would your uncle be?"

"Walter Richmond. He and my aunt run the Berry Grove Bed and Breakfast off of Portage Road."

"Oh, Walter!" Rebecca exclaimed. "Why, I didn't realize you had a family member with us. Isn't that just wonderful? So I guess that makes you an extended part of the Shopwells family, doesn't it?"

"Uh, sure."

"Come on, let's have a chat up in my office," Rebecca said, laying a gentle hand on Sherri's back to steer her away from the cafeteria. "You can park your cart right over here and everything will be waiting for you when we're finished."

"Great."

# CHAPTER SEVEN

SHERRI FOLLOWED REBECCA THROUGH A SET OF DOUBLE DOORS at the back of the store marked SHOPWELLS ASSOCIATES ONLY. Inside was a dim warehouse stacked with boxes still on skids and pallets. Racks of clothing still in plastic lined the walls, while one area seemed just reserved for the colour-coded hangers that the clothes would be transferred to. It was quieter here and, without the incessant muzak, Sherri felt her head begin to clear.

"The management offices are just up this way," Rebecca said, as she mounted a narrow metal staircase up to a second floor area, through another door and into a long bright hallway. Rebecca's heels clicked on the white tile as Sherri followed her. It looked so bright and clean that it reminded Sherri more of a hospital than an office.

"It's certainly different from the paper's offices," Sherri said, thinking of the homey old house with its creaking floors and dusty warmth. "It must have taken getting used to, a change like this . . ."

"Perhaps a bit," Rebecca said. "But everyone here was so welcoming. We really are like a large family. Now, here we have our general manager's and assistant manager's offices as well as some meeting rooms. I'm right near the end here."

Halfway down the hall, they passed a door that looked different from the other plain white office doors. This one was steel and marked PRIVATE in red letters.

"And what's in there?" Sherri asked, peering through the small square glass window. She glimpsed stainless steel counters, glass vials and what looked like an examination table.

"Oh, that's our health clinic," Rebecca said, ushering Sherri along. "We pride ourselves on the health care plan we provide for all our associates. We do everything on-site as well so that it's most convenient for the workers."

"So they don't have to take time out to leave work for medical attention?"

"We believe in preventative health care," Rebecca said. "We give every associate who joins us a flu shot and teach them about taking care of themselves, eating right, getting enough rest. A healthy employee is a happy employee."

Rebecca opened a door into a sleek, modern-looking office dominated by a long polished black desk. A flat screen TV on one wall was tuned to a twenty-four-hour news channel. Sherri wandered casually across to the large window behind Rebecca's desk. It looked down into the store, almost directly onto the customer service desk and main entrance.

"Nice. Can anyone see in here?" Sherri asked.

"No. From the sales floor this window just looks like a large mirror. So tell me, how do you like the community beat? I was happy covering municipal politics last summer, but I sometimes envied Krystal for being able to get out into the community so much and interact with people, get a real sense for the town." Rebecca lowered her voice and glanced around playfully, as if someone might be listening. "And, frankly, on the community beat you don't have to go to all those tedious political meetings. You're well away from those." Rebecca leaned back in her chair. "So what have you been working on so far?"

"Actually, Rebecca," Sherri said, opening up her notebook and uncapping her pen, "if you don't mind I'd love to ask *you* some questions."

"Sure thing."

"About Shopwells." Sherri reached into her purse, pulled out the small white digital recorder and laid it on the table between them. Only then did Rebecca's pleasant demeanor change. Her eyes narrowed.

"Sherri, forgive me, I'm a bit confused," Rebecca said, leaning back in her big leather chair. "I got the impression from your call that you wanted to talk about my work at *The Post*, that you wanted some tips and pointers."

"I don't need any tips on how to be a reporter. I wanted to ask *you* some questions." She moved to flick on the recorder. But a red light shone steady for only a second, then blinked and died.

"Oh dear," Rebecca said, her tone entirely unconvincing. "You must be out of batteries. Perhaps you'd like to pop down and buy some? Double As are fifty for five dollars today only."

"That's not necessary," Sherri said, taking up her pen and pad. "We can do this the old-fashioned way."

"All right then. So what can I tell you?"

"Well, to start with: what prompted you to stop reporting on Shopwells and start reporting *to* them?"

"Are you looking for advice on a career change, Sherri?" Rebecca purred.

"No. I'm happy as a reporter."

"Well, I was happy too until I saw a new opportunity. That's really all there is to it. So tell me, are you here on an assignment? Did Mac ask you to do this interview?"

"I'm here for a story."

"Well that's not exactly the same thing, is it? Are you here as a reporter with an assignment, or are you freelancing? Because something tells me that Mac wouldn't have put you up to this, so . . ."

"A story is a story. All I'm asking is to hear Shopwells' side of things. I'd rather get the story from the source than listen to rumours, and I'm sure you would prefer that as well."

"Of course. But there has to be something there to begin with."

"Let's begin with you. Your move from *The Post* to Shopwells raised some eyebrows. Everyone tells me you were investigating Shopwells real estate transactions before you made the switch."

Rebecca muted the television, then hit another button on the remote control. All of a sudden, the same muzak from the sales floor flooded the office. The buzzing in Sherri's ears returned and, for a moment, dizziness took hold again.

"I'm sorry, what was your question?" Rebecca asked.

Sherri faltered. "It was . . . I . . ." Her brow felt clammy. Then she started furiously scribbling on her notepad.

Rebecca sat back in her chair with a placid smile on her face.

After a long silence, Sherri looked up from her notepad

and said, "I was going to ask you about . . ." She tried to form the question, but her gaze shifted to the window behind Rebecca, to the sales floor, and her mind drifted back to an apple-green lamp she had seen earlier. *Maybe I should have grabbed it. What if there aren't any left by the time I finish here?*

"I'll tell you what," Rebecca said. "I have another meeting that I must get to. But I'm going to prepare a statement and send it over to you this afternoon." She opened the top drawer of her desk and peeled a coupon from a pad. "Now, don't tell anyone *I* gave this to you, but here's a coupon for thirty percent off your entire purchase today. After all, you are practically a member of the Shopwells family. I'll see you out to the sales floor."

Everything seemed to blur together then. Sherri was only vaguely aware of how Rebecca kept close behind her as they walked back out into that blinding white hallway and down the metal staircase into the dim silent warehouse.

"Thank you for taking the time to come out and see me," Rebecca said.

"But I . . ." The list of questions swirled in Sherri's head. She wanted to ask them all. She wanted to plant her feet and refuse to leave until Rebecca answered everything. But she was so dizzy that it felt somehow impossible to pluck one question out of the jumble in her head.

"You should get yourself something to eat. You do look a bit pale." Rebecca peered into Sherri's face. "Pop back to the cafeteria before you leave. Try the staff special. It's usually reserved for the associates, but tell them I said it's all right. I think it will do you some good."

"Thank you," Sherri heard herself say. "I just may do

that . . ." Then Sherri heard the clicking of Rebecca's heels on the stairs heading back up to the second floor, then the click as the door to the management offices shut.

Sherri was alone in the warehouse at the door to the sales floor. She moved to head back to the cafeteria, but then stopped herself. *Girl, what are you doing?* The staff special, Rebecca had said. That tweaked something in Sherri's mind. But she couldn't focus on exactly what. Was it something about Uncle Walter? Her mind had drifted again to that apple-green lamp . . .

*Stop. Breathe.* Sherri leaned against a shelf stacked with boxes wrapped in cellophane. *Now focus. You let it get away from you. What's wrong with you?*

Sherri moved to take a step toward the exit when the door burst open with such force that the knob slammed into the cinder block wall and sent a tremor through the stacks of boxes. Sherri ducked behind a rack of girls' party dresses and watched.

"This conversation is over!" hissed a tall man clad all in black who led the way.

"Like hell it is!" countered the second man, following close behind.

Sherri recognized them both from the framed photos hanging behind the customer service counter. The manager looked even more gaunt and bony in the flesh. Standing more than six feet high and with a slight hunch in his back that looked almost like a hump, he reminded Sherri of Ichabod Crane from the *Legend of Sleepy Hollow* cartoon she used to watch every Halloween as a kid. The assistant manager looked angry; he stalked after the manager, his face flushed. They seemed to be continuing an argument that had started out on the sales floor. The assistant manager still strained to keep his voice low here in the dim backroom, but he sounded more like he was hissing. Spittle shot out of his mouth.

"No. You listen to *me*, PK: I don't care if head office *has* authorized it," the assistant manager said. "These are people, not robots, and you're messing with their lives."

Sherri's eyes widened. In the shadows, she silently uncapped her pen and scribbled down everything she heard. If only the recorder was working, she could have had it all word for word.

"This comes from the top, Tom. You know that. You've *always* known that. You signed the forms . . . and everything else. You agreed." In his black suit the manager was almost lost in the shadows. His voice sounded icy cold with barely contained anger.

"Maybe I did, PK," Tom said. "But that was before I realized what it's really doing to people. Isn't there some alternative?"

For a moment Sherri held her breath. She stopped scribbling, afraid that even the faint scratching of her pen on the paper might be heard in the tense silence between the two men.

"You're not looking well," Peterson said finally. "You're obviously under a lot of stress. You'd better come upstairs to the health clinic so we can take a look at you."

"No. I'm fine," Tom said in a firm voice.

"Just a quick checkup," Peterson said. "It will only take five minutes, and I promise you'll feel a lot better."

Sherri almost couldn't breathe, watching. She leaned in closer to try and get a better look and knocked over a stack of boxes. Peterson's head snapped in her direction.

"Who's there?" he called, his voice echoing.

Sherri held her breath.

Peterson took a step in her direction. Then another.

The pen slipped from Sherri's hand and clattered to the floor. She froze, although a part of her wanted to leap out of the darkness, stick her recorder into Peterson's face—he didn't know if it was working or not—and bombard him with questions. But another voice, a calmer voice, told her to keep still. Sherri braced herself for discovery. But then the doors to the sales floor swung open and two workers in orange vests led in a half-dozen men and women in street clothes.

"Oh, excuse me, Mr. Peterson, Mr. Willard. I have some new recruits here," said the young woman in the orange vest. "I'm taking them to their orientation."

"Excellent," Willard said with a tremor in his voice as he sidestepped the group and moved toward the doors. "See you later, PK. Welcome aboard, everyone." He slipped out onto the sales floor.

"Tom, wait!" Peterson went after him.

Sherri quickly scurried around a corner, down another aisle, and ducked closer to the door. She peeked out between a rack of clothing and watched until the group of new recruits disappeared up the stairs to the second floor. Then she bolted from her hiding place onto the sales floor, with its cacophony of muzak and voices.

Suddenly a smiling Shopwells worker stepped into her path. The old woman's face was so wrinkled she reminded Sherri of a piece of withering fruit. "Well hello there, dear. Have you had a look through our *lingerie* department yet?

Lots of wonderful specials today," she said, lowering her voice on the word "lingerie" as if it were a four-letter word.

"No. I'm sorry, but I have to . . ." Sherri tried to slide past, but the woman held her ground.

"Oh, now you must take a look at these," the old lady said, placing a four-pack of underwear in Sherri's hand. "They're discounted fifteen percent today, and they are everything a practical young lady needs."

Sherri wanted to shove the old lady aside and bolt for the front doors. But she felt suddenly transfixed by the package in her hand. The young model prancing around on the label looked like she belonged on a beach down south somewhere, but the underwear she wore looked ridiculous, what the girls at school would call "granny panties." No teenaged girl would be caught dead wearing something so lame in the change room for gym. Sherri figured they would probably stretch up to her armpits if she got into a pair.

"They are a good price, aren't they?" Sherri heard herself say. "I guess I could use some practical things." She tucked them under her arm.

"And what have we here?" the elderly lady said, reaching for a package of ankle socks. They were trimmed with frilly lace and looked like something a five-year-old would wear to church with a pair of polished Mary Janes. "Five pairs for $4.99. And they're so dainty, aren't they?"

"They *are* cute," Sherri said, accepting the package.

"That's what you were looking for, wasn't it, my dear? And how about a nice flannel nightgown?" the old lady said, taking down a red and green plaid number with a frilly collar that looked like someone had vomited Christmas cheer all over it.

"It'll keep you cozy on those cold northern nights."

"It's perfect," Sherri said, taking the floor-length gown and draping it over her arm. "There was a lamp I wanted," Sherri told the woman. "A green lamp."

"Certainly, certainly! Let's head over to housewares. But let's get you a cart first."


The next half-hour was a jumble, and then the old lady led her to the checkout counter. "Have a nice day, dear," the woman said. "Thank you for shopping well at Shopwells."

"That will be $122.87," the woman behind the register said in a cheery voice. "Is that a coupon you have there?"

Sherri glanced down at the coupon in her hand. "Oh, I guess it is." She handed it over.

"Oooh," the cashier said. "I don't see too many of these. You must be a VIP! That'll be $86.01. A savings of more than thirty-six dollars!"

Sherri beamed, took her purchases in two giant orange shopping bags and headed for the exit. As the automatic doors glided open, a familiar voice called:

"Bye now! Thanks for shopping well at Shopwells!"

Sherri turned back and froze. Douglas stood there. He waved goodbye to all the departing shoppers. "Bye now. Goodbye! Have a great afternoon! Thanks for shopping well at Shopwells!" If he recognized Sherri, he gave no indication of it.

Sherri half-walked, half-stumbled across the parking lot to her car, and with every step away from the store, her head cleared a little bit more. But her confusion grew. As she approached the Mini, dug the keys from her pocket and tossed the bags and her purse in the back seat, she heard someone shout, "Hey, look out!"

Sherri turned and saw an abandoned shopping cart barrelling toward her. She leaped out of the way in time to see the cart slam into the side of the Mini. Sherri stumbled and fell forward. Pain shot up through her knee. She looked down to see a nasty scrape through a tear in her pants. But the cut on her knee was nothing compared to the giant dent in the driver's side door of the Mini. "Oh shit! Uncle Walter is going to flip!"

"Are you all right, miss?" called a man's even, emotionless voice. As Sherri eased herself to her feet, she saw Douglas striding toward her across the parking lot. His face looked blank as he glanced from the cart to Sherri and back again. "I'm afraid that one got away. This is why we encourage customers to return shopping carts to the store. On a windy day they can really zoom."

"*I* wasn't using a cart!"

"Then you should be more alert."

Sherri was livid. "Look what it did to my car!" Sherri said, pointing at the giant dent and the scratched paint.

Douglas' face remained impassive as he raised an index finger to a big blue sign on a nearby pole: PARK AT YOUR OWN RISK.

"You should always know about the dangers in your environment," Douglas said. "They can strike at any time. I'm afraid we can't do anything about your car, but we can take care of that nasty scrape on your knee. I'll take you to our health clinic and our doctor will fix you up in a jiff."

"No," Sherri said, opening the door and getting in. "I have to get back to the office."

"Thank you for shopping well at Shopwells," Douglas said, waving and walking back toward the store.

When Sherri pulled up to the office, she realized she had been gone for well over an hour. Not the best way to make a good impression on her first day.

She reached into the back seat for her purse and saw the bright orange Shopwells shopping bags.

"What the *hell*?" Sherri said aloud. *What on earth was I thinking?* She started pulling items from the bags: granny panties, little-girl socks, an old-lady flannel nightgown, a can of oven cleaner, a family pack of Gravol, a single person margarita maker, a box of mothballs, something that looked like a blue neck pillow (Sherri had a vague recollection of thinking it would be good for her neck after long hours at the computer, writing) and an apple-green lamp.

*What did I do? What happened to the interview with Rebecca?* Sherri tore open her notebook and stared at the notes she had scribbled. Her words started off looking like gibberish, like a doctor's scribbled notes on a prescription pad. Then Sherri began to make out words:

- green lamp
- drain opener
- shaving lotion
- eye shadow

It was a shopping list.

She turned the page and saw that her notes from the warehouse made sense. *Thank God for that!* She pulled out her digital recorder to check that. She pushed the power button and fiddled with the keys. Nothing. Then she popped open the back compartment. There were no batteries in it. *Krystal!*

# CHAPTER EIGHT

**SHERRI HADN'T MADE IT ONE STEP PAST MAC'S OFFICE WHEN HIS** voice boomed out into the hall. His tone said trouble.

"Richmond? Can I see you in here, please?"

Sherri took a deep breath and walked in. "Sure, Mac. What's . . ." She was surprised to see Krystal seated in the chair opposite Mac's desk. They looked at her, then looked at each other. "Sorry I was a bit late coming back from lunch," Sherri said, trying to make her breath sound even. "I got a bit tied up."

"Did you have an accident?" Mac said, noticing the tear in her pant leg.

Sherri glanced down as if she'd just noticed it herself. "Oh, this? It's nothing," she said, and her gaze fell on Krystal. "You should see the other girl."

"Oh, this is ridiculous," Krystal said, getting to her feet to face Sherri eye to eye. "We know you went to Shopwells, Sherri."

"Krystal," Mac cautioned from his seat. "I told you I would handle this."

"It was lunchtime," Sherri said to Krystal. "I went to their cafeteria."

"And what did you have?" Krystal shot back.

"A hamburger," Sherri lied easily.

"Baloney!" Krystal snapped.

"No," Sherri said, deciding to play the smartass card to the hilt. "It really was a hamburger."

"I don't care about what you ate. You interviewed Rebecca," Krystal countered. "And you've already been told that Shopwells is *my* beat."

"Then cover it!" Sherri snapped.

"Mac, can you jump in here, please?" Krystal said, plunking back into her seat in frustration.

"Did Rebecca call you directly to tell you I popped by?" Sherri asked her.

"Rebecca called *me*," Mac cut in, glowering now. Sherri looked at Mac, startled at his tone. "It doesn't reflect well on this paper to have a junior reporter conducting unauthorized interviews with our biggest advertiser, and Rebecca as good as said so."

"She threatened to pull advertising?" Sherri asked. "That's a story right there."

"You had no business being there no matter what the story," Krystal interjected.

"I'm sorry that I didn't ask your permission, Mac. But there is something seriously weird going on in that place."

"Richmond, you shouldn't be poaching another reporter's beat. Please do as I've said and focus on the community. Where's your story on the farmers' market?"

"I'll have it on your desk in an hour."

"Good. Here, Krystal. Rebecca faxed this over." He handed her a page. "This is the info on Shopwells' community work that Sherri asked for."

"The hell I did!" Sherri said, then stared at the ground when both Mac and Krystal looked hard at her.

"Krystal, write me up a few paragraphs on this. It'll help smooth the whole thing over."

"Of course," Krystal said, taking the page from him.

"All right," Mac said. "That's enough drama for one day. Back to work. Both of you."

Krystal strode out in triumph, shoulders squared and a smug smile on her wrinkled lips. Sherri turned to go.

"Richmond?"

She turned back to face him. "Yeah, Mac?"

"I want you to know that . . ." Mac waited until they heard Krystal's office door close. "I know you're going to do well here. You have good instincts."

She stood there, hoping for something more. Mac looked like he wanted to speak, wanted to ask her something, but instead he swivelled back to face the computer and signalled for her to go.

After cleaning up her scraped knee in the washroom, Sherri went back to her office, fired up her computer and got started on the farmers' market story.

> Lewton's annual farmers' market kicked off with a disappointing start this week, as the ten-year-old market welcomed back only three of the eight vendors who usually offer their fresh fruits, vegetables and other homemade items to the people of Lewton . . .

When she finished the story, Sherri went to put it in the wire mesh basket marked *copy* outside Mac's closed office door. From inside she could hear him talking into the phone. He sounded exasperated.

"I know, Mrs. Madison, and I'm sorry that Jimmy wasn't at school the day our reporter took the photo, but we really can't run a *second* photo this long after the fundraiser . . ."

Sherri noticed a single page already lay in the copy basket. It was Krystal's story on Shopwells.

### Shopwells Keeps Giving Back to Lewton.

It wasn't a story. It was just a bunch of feel-good garbage about Shopwells' sponsorship of the elementary school's junior basketball team. The lead quote was attributed to Rebecca:

"This is one of the many ways that Shopwells is
working to give back to the community of Lewton."

"Rebecca's not the only one who's a PR flack," Sherri muttered, dropping her farmers' market story into the basket.

Halfway out of the ghostly downtown core, a brightly lit storefront stood out from the mostly darkened shop windows nearby. ANITA'S BOOKSHOP—New and Used Books. Sherri pulled up.

A lone blue pickup truck with a rusting bumper sat parked out front. Sherri stepped inside and inhaled the familiar smell of old books. A woman with stringy silver hair leaned over a glass display case of antique books, staring into a glossy celebrity magazine. She glanced up when the bell on the door chimed.

"Help you?"

"Do you have a copy of *Jane Eyre*?"

The woman thought for a moment. "I should. Check the classics shelf, right over there."

Sherri craned her neck and scanned the spines. "I don't think it's here," she said.

"I must have a copy," the clerk said, sliding off her stool. "Let me check the backroom for you."

"Thanks." Sherri leaned against the counter to wait. She felt like a tightly wound ball of nerves. She hoped that soaking in a nice hot bath and reading the adventures of Jane Eyre would help calm her down. As she looked back out at the Mini, she caught movement, then saw a familiar figure crossing the parking lot. *Ben!* Sherri caught her breath as she watched him and realized he was headed in her direction. He had a faded grey backpack slung over one shoulder, and as he stepped into the bookshop, he gave Sherri a half-grin.

"Hey there, Miss Reporter," Ben said, closing the door after him. "Not having a very good first day, are you?" He stepped up to the counter and rang the silver bell sitting there. *Ding.*

The clerk's voice called from somewhere in the back of the store. "I'll be right with you!"

"It's only me, Anita," Ben called back. "I've got your dinner order from the luncheonette."

"Oh, great," came the muffled reply. "Be out in a second!"

"So how did you know I'm not having a good day?" Sherri asked.

"I could see it in your eyes," Ben joked, leaning in close enough for Sherri to smell his aftershave. "They're very nice eyes, by the way."

"Thanks." Sherri blushed.

"And I could also see it in that giant dent in your car and the tear in your slacks."

"Well hey there, Ben," Anita said, returning to the front. "I'm sorry, miss," she said to Sherri. "I must have that book buried way in the back. But I know it's there. If you come back tomorrow I'll have had the time to move some stuff around and get it."

"Sure," Sherri said. "I'll come by in the morning."

Ben accepted the ten dollars Anita gave him for her order, and she slipped a two-dollar coin into his hand too. "That's for such speedy service, young man," she said.

"You're awesome, Anita." Ben smiled and pocketed the money. "At this rate I'll be retiring to a beach somewhere before I'm twenty-five."

"Be sure you take *me* along," Anita quipped.

"Who else? You know I'm a one-woman guy," he said and held the door open for Sherri. "See you later."

"Quite the ladies' man, aren't you?" Sherri joked as Ben followed her outside.

"You mean Anita?" he asked. "I'm allowed to see other girls."

Michael popped into Sherri's mind. Her eyes must have widened because Ben looked at her, concerned.

"You okay, Sherri? You look like you just remembered you left the stove on or something."

"I'm fine," Sherri said. "There's something I have to take care of when I get home tonight. Can I give you a lift back to the luncheonette?" Sherri asked, leaning against the Mini.

"Thanks, but I like the walk," Ben said. "We don't have a heck of a lot of town to cross here, and besides, I'm not sure I can trust your driving. So what's with the dent?"

"Honestly? I was taken out by a runaway Shopwells shopping cart."

"What happened? You refuse a job offer?"

"Actually," she said, thinking of Douglas, "I guess I did."

Ben ran his calloused hands over the gouge, and when Sherri placed her hand on the scratched surface, her pinkie finger brushed against Ben's hand. From the corner of her eye, she saw him smile. "You could always take it to Mauricio's Body Shop. Tell him you're a friend of mine and he'll give you a good deal."

"Thanks. I guess you know everyone in town, huh?"

"Yeah, pretty much," Ben said. "They always say it's the therapists and hairdressers who have the goods on everyone. But they forget about waiters and delivery boys. We see everything."

Sherri sat on the hood of the Mini. For a moment she debated whether or not to say anything about her Shopwells suspicions, since it might leave him thinking she was a few sandwiches short of a picnic. Finally, Sherri said, "I have to ask you a question, and it's going to sound a little nutty."

"Okay . . ." Ben said, smiling as he slipped off his backpack and eased himself down next to her. "I like nutty. Sometimes I'm even partial to zany."

"First, though, no one in your family works at Shopwells, right? None of your friends?"

"Well, I *am* my family," Ben said. "My folks headed out west for a job transfer a few months ago, so I'm it. Most of the guys I went to school with either left town or work at Shopwells. They're the only ones hiring these days. Why the inquisition?"

"Do you think it's possible that Shopwells is like . . . some kind of cult?" She braced herself for Ben's laughter. But it never came.

"Well *of course* it's like a cult, Sherri. Have you seen the way the people in this town have glommed onto that place? It's nuts. I can hardly go an entire shift at the diner without someone trying to show me what they bought there, or one of my old school friends trying to recruit me to work there. So what?"

"No, I don't mean *like* a cult . . ." Sherri said, trying to clarify. "I mean it *is* a cult. Like, there is something seriously weird going on there. Just take a look at all this crap I walked out of there with!" She hopped off the hood, opened the back door and started pulling stuff out from the shopping bags.

"Nice underwear," Ben joked.

"No, they're not! They're hideous! So why the hell did I buy them?"

"You're hoping to start a hideous trend?"

"No, I couldn't help myself." Sherri threw the underwear back in the bag. "It's like I was being controlled, like I couldn't stop myself from buying everything they showed me. Haven't you felt that when you're in there?"

Ben shrugged. "To be honest, I steer clear of the place. I sort of wrote it off as people going overboard. It's a fad, right? It sweeps in, everyone gets caught up and for a while it's all anyone talks about. Pretty soon the novelty will wear off and people will stop being so nuts about the place."

"But how many fads do you know that can do *this* to a town?" Sherri said, indicating the empty storefronts around them. "Listen, there's more to it than I've told you . . ." Sherri took a deep breath and spilled it all: her wonky interview with Rebecca and her strange scribbled shopping list, the mounds of useless junk in Aunt Gillian's pantry and, finally, the confrontation between Tom Willard and the manager who looked like Ichabod Crane.

Ben had been sitting quietly as Sherri spoke, digesting everything she said. "Well you're right," Ben said finally. "That does sound kinda nutty. But I know Tom Willard. He used to run the hardware store, and he's a good guy. He actually gave me my first job stocking shelves when I was still in middle school. If something weird is going on at Shopwells, then Tom would be the one to speak out against it. He was a great boss."

"Then I've got to talk to Tom Willard."

"What about your uncle? If he works there too, he's bound to know something."

"I don't think so. Last night he . . ." Sherri shivered at the memory of Uncle Walter standing over her in the dark. "He was acting completely out of it. But then this morning it was like nothing had happened. Maybe that place is actually making people sick." She turned and saw Ben staring at her with a half-smile. "What is it?"

"Oh, nothing," Ben said. "It's cool watching as your mind pieces things together. Reminds me of a mousetrap ready to snap."

"Um . . . thanks, I think?"

"You're welcome. Here." He flipped open his cellphone. "Give me your number and I'll text you Tom's. I've got it right here."

"Awesome."

He tapped out the number. "There. Now you've got my number too."

They locked eyes for a moment and Ben gently took her hand. Sherri felt a tingling sensation dancing up the length of her arm.

"I wanted to ask you . . ." But a loud beeping interrupted him. "Damn," Ben said, dropping her hand.

Sherri awkwardly dug her hands into her pockets as Ben reached for his cell. "We don't have much luck with cellphones, do we?"

"They're out to get us," Sherri agreed, remembering Michael's ill-timed phone call that morning at the farmers' market.

"It's a text from Tony. Would you look at this?" Ben showed her the screen.

W%er8 are yPMu? I}ve got ano8dher o%$er for U to de%34er?

"What the hell does *that* mean?"

"He's saying: *Where are you, I've got another delivery for you.*"

"You speak gibberish? I'm impressed."

"Poor Tony. My biggest mistake was teaching that guy how to text. But he's never figured out how to make his phone do letters instead of numbers. It used to take me forever to decipher them, but now I've got it down to a science. But now he even texts me on my day off to ask what I'm doing."

"Better be sure to keep him off Facebook, then," Sherri teased.

"So he could stalk me there too? I don't think so." Ben pocketed his cellphone. "Still, I'd better dash." He slipped his bag back over his shoulder. "Drop by the luncheonette sometime when you're not dodging shopping carts."

"Sure."

"And let me know how it goes talking to Tom. I'll be curious to hear."

"I'm calling him as soon as I walk in the house."

# CHAPTER NINE

**BUT TOM WILLARD WAS NOT THE FIRST PERSON ON SHERRI'S** mind when she walked into the farmhouse. Instead, she kicked off her shoes, bolted up the stairs to her bedroom and dialled Michael in the city.

The thrill of her second encounter with Ben was now battling her growing sense of guilt over Michael. Already, Ben knew more about what was going on with her life here than her own boyfriend did. Sherri felt like she had somehow cheated on Michael by sharing her day with Ben first, like she'd robbed her boyfriend of the story somehow. Well, she would tell Michael all about it now, in even more detail than she'd given Ben. But Michael's cellphone rang and rang and rang. Voicemail picked up.

"It's me," Sherri said, trying to sound casual. "Sorry we didn't connect today. It was a really busy first day. I'd, uh, love to tell you all about it." Sherri pictured Ben's face again and heat flooded her. *Well, not all of it,* she thought. "I'll be up late, so call anytime. I miss you." She hung up.

"Sherri, dear!" Aunt Gillian's voice floated up the staircase. "Dinner will be ready soon. Come on down and tell me how the rest of your day as an ace reporter went. Did my jam make the front page?"

Sherri smiled to herself. Aunt Gillian may have been a bit nutty, a bit jam-happy, but she was still a sweetheart. "Down in a few minutes," Sherri called. First, she dialled Tom Willard.

"Hello?"

"Hi, is this Mr. Willard?"

The voice on the other end of the phone sounded automatically cagey, alert. Sherri heard him swallow audibly. "Who's *this*?" His words sounded slightly slurred, as if he had been drinking.

"Mr. Willard, I'm so sorry to bother you at home. My name is Sherri Richmond."

"Okay . . ." he said, relaxing slightly at her formal introduction. Maybe he thought she was a customer? "What can I do for you?"

"I need to ask you some questions about Shopwells."

Tom Willard snapped, suddenly on the offensive: "What do you want?"

"I was in the store today. I'm the new reporter with *The Post* and . . ."

*Click.*

Sighing, she dialled back. After five rings, Tom Willard picked up again, sounding exasperated.

"*What?*"

"Mr. Willard, please. I need your help to answer some questions. I'm a friend of Ben's, who used to work for you? He said you were a good boss and you would want to help. This afternoon you were arguing with the manager in the back warehouse area and . . ."

"Lady, please . . ." he said, lowering his voice to a whisper. Now it wasn't anger, but fear that Sherri heard in Tom Willard's voice. "*Please!* I can't talk to you about this stuff. I tried once and it didn't help. It only made things worse. I don't know how much you know about anything, but *please* leave me out of it, okay?" Then, speaking in a normal-toned, angry voice again, Tom Willard said, "No, I will not speak to anyone from the press. Shopwells policy is that all requests have to go through our PR manager. I suggest you call Rebecca Scott during regular business hours." Again he hung up.

Sherri attacked the plate of spaghetti and meatballs Aunt Gillian placed in front of her.

"My goodness, dear," her aunt said, unfolding a napkin into her lap and moving to spoon a portion of pasta onto her own plate. "Didn't you get enough lunch today?"

Sherri had to stifle a laugh. It came out sounding more like a choke, and Aunt Gillian reached over to pat her back. "Thanks," Sherri said, coughing. "No. I had to skip lunch. Too busy."

Aunt Gillian frowned. "That's not healthy at all! How is a growing girl supposed to keep her mind on her work without a good meal? You tell that Ted MacLachlan that you're to have a proper lunch hour or he'll have me to answer to." Aunt Gillian spooned an extra helping of pasta onto Sherri's plate for good measure.

"Thanks, Aunt Gillian," Sherri said, and smiled at the mental image of Aunt Gillian going toe-to-toe with Mac. As she chewed, Sherri stared at the empty seat where her uncle should have been sitting. "Uncle Walter not joining us again?"

Aunt Gillian shook her head. "Working late again."

"Aunt Gillian, has Uncle Walter ever told you anything about what it's like to work at Shopwells?"

"He tells me he loves it."

"I know. But has he ever mentioned anything out of the ordinary?"

"Like what, dear?"

From the dark living room behind them came the sound of scraping wood, as if someone had bumped into a piece of furniture. Sherri jumped in her seat and craned around to see Uncle Walter step out of the shadows.

"Well hello, ladies," he said, shuffling into the kitchen. He still wore the familiar orange vest, and Sherri felt herself stiffen involuntarily as he bent down to kiss the top of her head.

"Walter, dear!" Aunt Gillian shot up from her seat to kiss him on both cheeks. "Why are you home so early? How lovely! Sit, join us."

She bustled over to the kitchen cabinet as Uncle Walter slipped off his orange vest and hung it next to two others in the closet. Sherri felt relieved when he tucked it out of sight.

"They let me head out early tonight," Walter said, sitting down next to Sherri.

"Weren't things busy?" Aunt Gillian asked, returning with an extra plate for him.

"Hopping," Uncle Walter said. "But Mr. Peterson said they had things in the automotive department under control. Two new trainees started today."

Sherri remembered the group of new recruits who had shuffled into the back warehouse before Tom Willard stormed off.

Aunt Gillian moved to dish out a heaping portion of spaghetti for Uncle Walter. He held up a hand for her to stop. "No need, Jilly. I had my supper already."

"Oh, but, honey," Aunt Gillian pleaded. "I made it just the way you always used to like it. Have a little bite."

"Can't. Stuffed," he said, pouring a glass of water and drinking deeply. Then he turned to look at Sherri, his face suddenly serious. "Haven't you got something to tell us, young lady?"

*Something to tell him? Had Rebecca pulled him aside? I never should have told that woman Walter's my uncle.*

"Something about the car, maybe?" Uncle Walter said, raising an eyebrow.

"Right, that. I am *so* sorry. I was going to tell you as soon as you got home. I'll get it repaired out of my first paycheque. And a friend in town said he knows a good garage."

"What's all this, then?" Aunt Gillian said, looking between the two of them.

"I was in the parking lot and this shopping cart came out of nowhere."

"Now, now," Uncle Walter said firmly. He patted her hand. "You needn't worry. Rebecca told me that it wasn't your fault. And Shopwells is going to take care of it in their garage. But you need to take care yourself, dear."

For a moment their eyes locked and Sherri felt her heart sink.


**S**herri stood in front of her bedroom mirror looking at herself in the long-sleeved plaid fleece nightgown from Shopwells.

The tight collar half choked her and made her look like an old schoolmarm, while the hem practically reached to her ankles and the fabric itched her all over. She felt like a plaid sack of potatoes.

*Maybe Uncle Walter could take all this stuff back for me.* Sherri tugged the itchy nightgown over her head, tossed it into the Shopwells bag and slipped into the sweatpants and tank top she always wore to bed. It had been a long, crazy first day and every muscle in her body was beginning to ache as if she had run a marathon. But first, she padded barefoot down toward the main floor. As Sherri rounded the banister of the staircase, Aunt Gillian peeked out at her from the master bedroom. Her hair was rolled up in curlers and her face was already stripped of makeup. "Everything okay, dear?" Aunt Gillian asked in a low voice.

"Yeah," Sherri whispered. "I'm getting a glass of milk."

Aunt Gillian nodded. "If Uncle Walter is still in the living room, tell him to come up. The last time he fell asleep in front of the television, he woke up with a crick in his neck that didn't go away for nearly a month!"

"Sure, I'll tell him."

In the living room, the TV was on, but there was no sign of Uncle Walter. In the kitchen, Sherri was putting the carton of milk back in the fridge when she heard the groaning of floorboards overhead. Someone was walking in the hallway. On tiptoes, she crept up the staircase and down the long narrow hall. She stopped and flattened herself against the wall around the corner from the little end table with the rotary phone. Someone was twirling the old phone dial: *whirr, whirr, whirr . . .*

"It's me." It was Uncle Walter's voice, but he spoke so low that Sherri had to strain to hear. "Yes . . ." Uncle Walter said and paused as the person on the other end of the phone spoke. "Yes," he said again. "No. I don't think so. Yes, I'll keep an eye on her."

Sherri froze. Then she rounded the corner into the hallway, startling Uncle Walter, who quickly replaced the receiver without saying goodbye.

"Aunt Gillian told me you'd better be careful, Uncle Walter."

"What?"

"Your neck."

"Oh. That."

# CHAPTER TEN

SHERRI'S CELLPHONE RANG AT EIGHT, WAKING HER UP. SHE groaned and reached for it. "Hello?"

"Hey, it's Michael."

"Oh, hi," she said with forced cheerfulness.

"Sorry it's so early. But I thought I'd catch you before you went to work."

"I've been trying to reach you. Where have you been?"

"Me? Where have *you* been?"

"I've been right here," she said. "I called your cell and it kept going to voicemail. I texted you too."

"I've been busy."

"Seems like it. So how are things in Toronto?"

"Pretty much the same as you left them. But hotter. Lots of smog. How are things up there? Job going okay? Sounded like you were really involved when I called."

Sherri cringed, remembering how she'd hustled Michael off the phone so she could keep talking with Ben at the farmers' market. Had Michael heard Ben's voice? "I'm sorry," Sherri said. "I'm busy with this big story."

"Too busy to talk to your boyfriend?"

"That's not fair."

For a moment neither of them spoke. *Stalemate.* Finally, Michael said, "And here we are again."

"Looks like it." It felt exactly like their goodbye on the front porch of her parents' house—Michael sulking, Sherri fuming.

"This isn't why I called, Sherri. Really. I wanted to say I missed you."

"You could have started with that." Her voice lost some of its edge. If Michael was going to try, the least she could do was meet him halfway. "I miss you too," she added softly.

"And I was thinking I might come up to visit."

*Oh no. No, no no!* Sherri pictured the look on Michael's face if he saw the crumbling bed and breakfast and she had to explain the whole Shopwells thing. Worse still, she pictured Ben and Michael meeting on the street. She imagined having to introduce them.

"That could be nice," she said.

"Could be?"

"But maybe a little later in the summer. I'm so tied up with this story right now, I wouldn't be able to spend much time with you."

"I was hoping I could drive up there and we could . . ." He trailed off.

"Could what, Michael?" But she had a pretty good idea.

"Well, I thought we could do what we were planning to do after graduation?"

Sherri flushed. That's why they had argued before she left Toronto. Sherri had agreed to get a hotel room and spend the night together after the grad dance. But once she got the job in Lewton, she changed her mind. Sherri didn't want to sleep with Michael for the first time right before leaving for the whole summer. It wouldn't be a big deal, Michael had insisted. But it was a big deal—to Sherri. And now here it was again—the same proposition and the same fight.

"Michael, nothing's changed. You'd still have to go back to Toronto and I'd be here alone. That's not how I pictured our . . ." she lowered her voice, "our first time. It's not going to happen while I'm in Lewton."

"This has nothing to do with your new job," Michael said, his voice hard again. "If you really wanted to be with me, it wouldn't matter where you were living or what summer job you had. I don't think you actually *want* to be with me."

"Can you hear my eyes rolling? I've given you my answer, okay? What are you going to do next? Double-dog dare me to sleep with you, Michael?"

"You always turn important things into a joke."

"This isn't a joke and it is important to me," Sherri snapped. "Very important, actually, and so are you. And that's why I want to wait until we're back together again and not have some kind of one-night stand in a cheap motel room!"

But even as Sherri said the words, it hit her. Michael was right. *Shouldn't I be excited to have him drive up for a romantic weekend?* A lingering doubt began to twist itself in the pit of her stomach.

"Fine. I hear you, okay?" Michael said. "It's just that seven weeks is a long time."

"You'll live," Sherri assured him.

"Well how about if I come up for just a visit?" Michael

suggested. "We could stay at your aunt and uncle's. Separate rooms and everything."

"Sure, but not for a bit. I told you, I've got a lot of things going on. Now, I've really got to go. I have to get ready for work."

"I got it. Listen, Sherri. There's something else I wanted to tell you. The last couple of times you called, I was out with Anna."

Sherri felt as if she had been punched in the gut. An image of Anna Cameron's scrunched up little face and perky blonde bobbed hair flashed in her mind. Anna Cameron of the cheerleading squad. Anna Cameron who probably weighed no more than thirty pounds soaking wet. Anna Cameron, a.k.a. Michael's girlfriend through all of junior year, and the girl he'd lost his virginity to.

"Okay . . ." Sherri said slowly. "You mean you guys have been hanging out in a group or . . ."

"No," Michael said carefully, and Sherri realized from his tone that he must have been debating whether or not to tell her this from the moment she had picked up the call. "Well, she came over to watch a movie the other night. And last night we went out for a bite."

"You had *dinner* together?"

"We've been friends since kindergarten, Sherri."

"I have friends from kindergarten too, Michael. But I haven't gone to bed with any of them!"

"Look, she heard you had taken the job out of town for the summer. She knew I'd need the company."

"And I'm sure you told her what kind of company you were looking for. Okay, so why are you telling me this?"

"I wanted to be honest with you. I'm not stupid, Sherri. I knew you'd come back and hear that Anna and I had been hanging out. And now, since I'm probably not coming to visit—"

"You'll be hanging out *more*? So I'm the big bad girlfriend, right? And if I don't invite you up here, you'll make Anna your summer girlfriend? You going to go rent that motel room with her instead of me? Is that your ultimatum?"

"This isn't an ultimatum. Stop sounding so crazy. Look, maybe I'm not saying this right."

"Understatement of the year. You've said enough. I have to get ready for work. Give Anna my regards when you see her tonight."

"Sherri, c'mon. Don't be like this."

"Have a nice summer, Michael." She hung up.


**S**herri was still fuming about Michael on her drive into Lewton. But she forgot all about him the moment she pulled up to Anita's Bookshop.

"What the hell?" Anita's was closed down. Newsprint plastered the front windows, and the glowing neon sign had been removed so only silver wires snaked down over the door. It had barely been twelve hours since she'd stood in this store with Ben. Sherri sat and stared. Her eyes darted from page to plastered page. They weren't newspapers at all. They were Shopwells flyers. She leaped out of the car.

Sherri tried to peer inside, but she couldn't get a look. The flyers completely covered the glass. They had been pasted together at perfect right angles.

"Hello?" Sherri called through the windows. She knocked a fist against the glass. Silence.

As she turned back toward the deserted parking lot, Sherri scanned the surrounding storefronts. Every one was empty. All of their front windows were plastered over with Shopwells flyers.

Sherri burst into Tony's Luncheonette. A lone diner picked at his half-eaten plate of pancakes. In front of a long Formica dining counter, a rotund little man in a white apron stopped sweeping and looked up at her.

"Is Ben here?" Sherri asked, breathless.

"Gave him the day off," the man in the apron said. "Can I help you with something?"

Sherri shook her head and tried to compose herself. "No. No, thanks." She glanced warily at the lone diner. *Did I see him working at Shopwells?* She tried to picture him in an orange vest and couldn't be sure.

"You must be Sherri," the man in the apron said, stepping forward to offer his beefy hand. "Ben's mentioned you. I'm Tony."

"Hi, Tony," Sherri said.

"Ben's in tomorrow for the lunch shift. But sometimes he calls in to see if there's extra work he can pick up. If he does, I'll let him know you came by."

"Thanks. I'll try his cell," Sherri said, turning to go.

"How are you liking our little town?" Tony called after her.

Sherri suppressed a manic laugh. "It's getting more interesting every day."

Outside, she dialled Ben, but all she got was an automated voice. "The customer you are dialing is unavailable. Please, try again later."

Mac's office door was closed, but Sherri heard his keyboard clicking. She was tempted to go in, but thought better of it. He had already made it clear that he didn't want to hear more about what was happening to the shops downtown.

A sheet of paper covered in red ink lay on her desk. It was her story on the Lewton Farmers' Market. Corrections littered the page. Whole sentences were crossed out, leaving barely a paragraph of text. Big, bold, red letters at the bottom read: *See me*. Mac's writing.

Sherri strode in without knocking. "What's with the hatchet job?" She dropped the story on the table.

But it was Krystal, not Mac, who swivelled in Mac's chair to face Sherri. She looked like a spy movie villain turning to confront her nemesis. All she needed was a monocle and a vicious-looking cat perched in her lap.

But the only cat around was on Krystal's powder-blue sweatshirt, a fluffy orange kitten hanging by its front paws from a laundry line. Sherri pictured that same sweatshirt on Goldfinger and suppressed a smile.

"Mac's at a meeting," Krystal said, leaning forward.

"Okay, but why are you in his office?"

"I'm glad you came in," Krystal said. "Mac asked me to tweak your story and go over it with you." She handed Sherri a clean sheet. "I printed out the edited version."

Sherri scanned the page:

Lewton's farmers' market kicked off another exciting season last week at the exhibition lot on Main Street south of Brunel Road. On offer this week were fresh honey, preserves and organic plants from some of our locals. The farmers' market will be open every Wednesday from 10:00 a.m. to 2:00 p.m. Be sure to visit!

Sherri was shaking her head by the time she got to the end of the short piece.

"Something funny?" Krystal asked.

"Not *ha ha* funny," Sherri said. "This isn't a tweak. This is a rewrite, and not a very good one. There are no names, no details—you took out everything that made this interesting."

"Don't try to tell me my business, Sherri. I've been a reporter since before you were born."

Sherri slapped the new sanitized story back onto the desk. "This isn't even a story."

"We've decided it works best as a cutline for your photo, and it will appear on page sixteen," Krystal said calmly.

"So you rewrote it *and* you're burying it!"

"I cut everything that doesn't belong on the community page. Sherri, I know this whole scrappy reporter persona is your thing, but this isn't *His Girl Friday*."

Sherri stalked back to her office. She wanted to throw something down the hallway. She paced the short length of her office, trying to calm down.

*Damn, why wasn't Ben at work this morning?* He was the only one in this crazy town who listened to her.

She heard the front door shut and Mac's voice downstairs. "Morning, Viv. Any mail?"

"Already put it in your inbox, Mac."

Sherri bolted from her desk in time to see Mac appear on the landing.

"Morning, everyone," he called out.

She froze when she saw him holding a bright orange Shopwells bag and a cardboard drink tray with three orange Shopwells coffee cups.

"Morning, Richmond," Mac said. "I see we didn't scare you off on your first day," he joked, backing into his office. "Did you need something?"

"I want to talk to you about my farmers' market story," Sherri said.

Krystal slipped out from behind Mac's desk. "I already handled that for you, Mac, just like you asked." Krystal met Sherri's stare and held it. "Did you bring us a treat, Mac?"

"I did," he said, setting everything on his desk. He handed a coffee to Krystal and another to Sherri, who eyed it warily.

"You do drink coffee, right, Richmond?"

"Sure I do," Sherri said. But she had no intention of drinking *that* coffee. "But I've already met my caffeine quota for the morning, thanks."

Mac tossed the drink tray into his overflowing recycling bin. "I showed Rebecca your story, Krystal. She liked it. We're all on the same page again. Good work."

"Thanks," Krystal said, smirking at Sherri.

Sherri had to bite her lip to keep from snapping. "So, Mac, about my farmers' market story," she said, sliding into the seat opposite his desk. She shot Krystal a look that said: *You can leave us alone now*. But Krystal stayed put.

"It's been taken care of," Mac said, digging into his Shopwells bag. He pulled out a travel-sized hair dryer, a set of jumper cables and one of those plastic fish on a plaque. It burst into song when he set it on the desk. Finally, he brought out a familiar-looking Styrofoam takeout container. Sherri caught her breath at the sight of it.

A phone sounded from down the hall. Mac glanced down at the blinking red light on his own phone. "That's your line, Krystal," he said.

For a moment Krystal hesitated, then, with a glare at Sherri, she walked out into the hall to her office, calling out, "I'm coming, I'm coming!"

"Richmond," Mac said, "I have your morning assignment. Should be fun—it's the end-of-year music competition at the high school. Be sure to get lots of photos."

"Is Krystal going to rewrite this one too?"

"Not if you stick to the subject instead of writing about how the town is shutting down."

"But it *is* shutting down! I was at Anita's bookstore last night and today it's closed. How strange is that? Tell me there isn't a story there."

"Stores close down, Richmond. It's sad, but it happens."

"But why did it close? Why are there Shopwells flyers in the window? And who owns the store now? If Shopwells is buying up all the real estate to put the local merchants out of business, that's a big story, Mac."

"Hold on a second, Richmond," he said, sighing. "I can never argue on an empty stomach." He popped open the lid to the Styrofoam container.

Sherri shuddered as Mac spooned a heaping portion of the staff special into his mouth. "You eat that for breakfast?"

"Food is food, Richmond. Now, listen to me. I used to be just like you."

"You used to be a teenage girl?"

"I used to be a young reporter," Mac said. "And I wanted to make it in the big leagues too. I know someone like you isn't planning to stay in a place like this for long. You've got a good head on your shoulders. You ask the right questions and you know a good story when you see it."

"Thanks."

"But you have to learn when to back off." He leaned back in his chair, folded his hands over his stomach and stared up at the ceiling. "I started off as a cub reporter at *The Observer*."

"Wow. Why did you leave?"

"You mean, what am I doing at a small-town paper when I started off in the big city? Usually it goes the other way around, right?" Mac half-smiled. "The newsroom at *The Observer* was something right out of a movie. There was a permanent yellow cigarette haze hanging in the air. Everyone worked on these giant black Remington typewriters. When deadline rolled around you had to shout to be heard over everyone banging at the keys at once. So there I was, not much older than you are now."

Mac spooned another helping of staff special into his mouth, chewed, swallowed and licked the spoon. "Did you have breakfast yet? Plenty here for two."

"No, thanks. I'm fine," Sherri said, grimacing. "So what did you cover at *The Observer*?"

"I started at the bottom, just like you're doing. I did the

night shift, listening in on the police scanner. I even covered the International Scrabble Tournament when it came to Toronto. But one day a real story—a big story—came my way. I was just like you. Dogged. But it didn't serve me well. That story happened to be about one of our biggest advertisers and their dirty tricks to bust their workers' union. The story ran on page one, and they pulled their ads. Same day, my editor and I were marched into the publisher's office and given pink slips. That's how this world works, Sherri. After that, no big paper would hire me. I've been in Lewton ever since. So let me ask you something, Richmond. Who's our biggest advertiser?"

"Okay, I get your point. But you did the right thing back then and you know it. It's your publisher who was wrong—the paper should have stood by you."

"That's not the way it works when money's involved. Maybe you've got a good story here, but it's not a good story for *The Lewton Leader-Post*. Do you understand what I'm telling you?"

"I understand, Mac. Thanks. Just one question, though."

"What?"

"How far did Rebecca get on this story?"

"You can read all about it in the morgue," Mac said, frowning. "But on your own time—not ours. Now you'd better get over to the Lewton High School. The competition starts at ten."

# CHAPTER ELEVEN

SHERRI WONDERED WHY EVERY HIGH SCHOOL SMELLED EXACTLY
the same. Perhaps it was the combination of industrial strength
cleaners, girls' cheap perfume, boys' gym clothes and the
greasy smell of french fries and heat-lamp pizza. She walked
through a long hallway lined with dented green lockers where
hand-painted posters and banners advertised the BATTLE OF
THE BANDS. Sherri followed the sound of guitars being tuned,
to a pair of double doors that led to the cafetorium.

"Check. Check," a skinny boy with long hair dangling
over his pimply face spoke into a microphone at the centre of
the stage. "Check, check one, check two. Hey, I think we've
got it now!"

A sharp jolt of feedback crackled, and everyone in the
room covered their ears and winced.

"C'mon guys! Get it together," a familiar voice called. "We
go on in twenty minutes!"

*Ben!* He had an acoustic guitar draped around his shoulder.
He strode across the stage and crouched down to tinker with
an amplifier.

"Ben," Sherri called.

He turned and smiled broadly. "Check it out, guys. The media showed up!" Everyone on the stage turned to stare at Sherri. "We've got to rock it if we want to make the front page, guys."

The band laughed as Sherri walked onto the stage.

"You're in a band, Ben?" Sherri asked. "You're not still in school, are you?"

Ben gave her a look. "For your information, I graduated last year. But the buddies I used to play with are all busy working at you-know-where, so now I play with these guys."

"What's your band called?" Sherri asked, looking at the band names painted on a banner above the stage. "Wait—there are only two? Isn't that more like a *duel* than a battle?"

"Ha ha. We're called Good Dog."

"I tried to get you on your cell this morning."

"Can't get enough of me, huh?" Ben smiled.

"That must be it. Don't you have voicemail?"

Ben shrugged. "Can't afford it. What's up?"

"A ton!"

"Uh oh," Ben said. "Did your uncle freak about the car?"

"Forget the car. Did you see Anita's this morning? It's closed. *Closed.* Like everything else on Main Street."

"Holy shit."

"Hey, language!" called a teacher who stood in the wings of the stage, cradling a clipboard.

"Sorry, Miss Kyle," Ben called. He hopped off the stage and led Sherri into a corner, where they couldn't be overheard. "Tony's not going to be happy. Anita was one of the few regulars we had left."

"The windows of the bookshop—the windows of *all* the shops that are closed down—are plastered with Shopwells flyers."

"Great. The people of Lewton have finally caught on to the whole reuse, recycle thing," Ben said, trying to lighten the tone.

Sherri rolled her eyes.

"Hey, Ben—we need you to come check this out," a boy called from the stage. "Something's weird with this amp!"

"Sure," Ben replied. He turned back to Sherri and touched her arm. "Can we talk about this later? We're going on any minute now." He leaped back onto the stage.

The first wave of students flooded in, shouting and laughing. Sherri dragged a folding chair into a corner and sat down. As the seats filled and the lights dimmed, Sherri held her bulky camera at the ready.

Pink Denim was up first. They were a quartet of girls with heavy eye makeup wearing pink, short pleated skirts. They crooned a couple of pop tunes. The boys in the audience whistled and hollered. Sherri snapped a few pictures of the lead singer pouting at the crowd. She had to admit, they were pretty good.

Then it was time for Good Dog.

Sherri lowered her camera when Ben stepped out on stage. A couple of girls in the audience cheered: "Woo hoo! Shake it, Ben!"

"Our first song is 'I Want You So Bad, Girl'. I just wrote it. I hope you guys like it." Ben launched into the opening riff. Sherri held her breath.

It all crashed and burned from there. Poor Ben! It sounded

like he was playing the guitar with sausages instead of fingers. And his voice! How could a guy with such a sweet voice be such a rotten singer? The lyrics made Sherri cringe, and Ben couldn't even keep in tune with his backup singer. And the drummer lost one of his sticks during a solo. He had to scamper into the wings for another.

Dutifully, Sherri snapped photo after photo—thankful that the camera couldn't record Ben's voice. A headline leaped into her mind: *Good Dog Needs to be Put Down.*

Mercifully, their performance didn't last long. They only got through two songs before Ben's backup singer actually managed to forget the words to the third one. Ben glanced over his shoulder and fell silent. The music sputtered and died.

"Uh, thanks, everyone," Ben said, amidst a smattering of applause and snickers. "We'll, uh, we'll be playing again throughout the summer. Look for us."

"Where? In the doghouse?" a girl sitting near Sherri shouted out.

Sherri's heart broke a little for Ben as Good Dog slinked off the stage.

Finally, a tubby man in a brown tweed jacket and a yellow shirt ambled awkwardly onto the stage. *The principal.*

"Well wasn't that great, everyone?" he said. "Now it's time to decide our winner."

*Oh man, do we have to?*

"By applause, let's hear it. Who won this year's battle of the bands for Lewton High?" The crowd went nuts when the teenyboppers from Pink Denim pranced back out on the stage, blowing kisses. Then Good Dog reappeared, all of them slump-shouldered and embarrassed, except Ben who beamed at the crowd. Maybe a dozen people clapped half-heartedly.

The principal presented the girl band with a wooden plaque, and everyone got up to go. Sherri weaved through the crowd to snatch a few quotes from the students as they flooded toward the door. A small semicircle of students formed around her at the sight of her camera and notepad.

"What did you think of the show?" Sherri asked.

"So lame," said one girl.

"Pink Denim were sorta okay," said another, cracking a big wad of blue bubble gum in her mouth.

"But Good Dog needs to give it up."

A chorus of giggles erupted.

"Yeah, they should change their name to Dead Dog!"

"What did you think, Sherri?" Ben asked, walking up to her.

"Well everyone in the crowd had a blast."

Ben smirked. "They're happy not to be in class. What about you? You gonna give us a rave review?" Ben grinned as he pushed the hair out of his eyes. Sherri laughed, until she realized Ben wasn't joking.

"Oh, um, it won't actually be a *review*, just some details about the event." She looked down at the linoleum.

"So you thought we sucked, is that it?"

"Ben, c'mon, let's forget about it."

"I know we had some sound problems, but you should hear us when everything hangs together. We're not horrible. We just had a bad day."

"I didn't say you were horrible."

"You didn't have to," Ben said, returning to the stage to

pack up his gear. "You should have seen the look on your face after the show. I guess you're used to the big city sounds, huh?" Ben said, looking genuinely hurt.

"It's just a high school show."

Ben snatched up his guitar case and stormed out.

"Ben, wait!"

But he didn't turn around.

As Sherri started the Mini, her cellphone rang. She rummaged for it, hoping it was Ben. But Michael's name flashed on the screen. Sherri hit the ignore button and tossed the phone into the passenger seat. The voicemail light blinked. Sherri reached for the phone and listened to Michael's message.

> Hey, it's me. Look, I'm calling to say I'm sorry about this morning. And I'm not gonna hang out with Anna anymore. I miss you and want to spend time with you this summer. Call me and let's figure out how we can make this happen.

"Not good enough." Sherri deleted the message.

"How did the Battle of the Bands go?" Mac asked, stepping into her office.

"It was okay. Great."

"Think you can pull the copy together quickly? It will need to be proofed, and the paper goes to print at the end of the day."

"I'm on it," Sherri said, sliding behind the computer.

"Deadline's in an hour and after that you can take the rest of the day off. Not much going on this afternoon."

"Okay."

She took a breath and wrote a rave review of Good Dog:

> Good Dog stormed the stage at Lewton High's Battle of the Bands Thursday. Lead singer Ben Quinlan wowed the crowd with his original song, "I Want You So Bad, Girl." Good Dog's follow-up, "Girl, I Need You So Bad," whipped the crowd into a frenzy. Look out, Lewton. These young men have a future on the stage. Meanwhile, girl-band Pink Denim won the competition with their covers of Britney Spears songs.

A few minutes after she filed the piece and a matching photo, Mac wandered into her office with the printed story in his hand. He was smiling.

"This is good work, Richmond," he said.

"Yeah? Thanks." Sherri kept her gaze down. *What a strange place. A real story gets shelved, but a complete lie is "good work."*

"This is exactly the kind of thing I was talking about, what was missing from your farmers' market piece: upbeat. Community friendly. Nicely done."

"Thanks, Mac," Sherri said.

"I've one question," Mac said, sitting down opposite her. "You know that you buried your lead, right?"

"Sorry?" Sherri asked as if she had no idea what he was talking about.

"Well the lead should be who *won* the competition. But you don't mention that Pink Denim won until your final sentence."

"So are you going to make me rewrite it?" Sherri asked.

"Naw, it'll be fine. But the photo you submitted," Mac said, holding up a printout. "You also decided to feature the losing band in the photo—in particular the lead singer. Anything you'd like to tell me?"

Sherri shrugged. "The photos of the first band didn't turn out so well."

Mac looked at her skeptically.

"Fine, if you want to know the truth, all the girls in the first band were wearing super short skirts. I was shooting from below the stage. I figured you wouldn't want the Penny Potters in this town freaking out over some massive wardrobe malfunction in the community pages. Imagine our readers sitting down with their coffee tomorrow morning and looking at a giant—"

Mac held up his hands for her to stop. "That's quite all right, Richmond. I don't need details, and neither will Penny Potter. We'll use this photo. Good work."

Sherri smiled. At least she was getting something right today, even if it was totally wrong.

# CHAPTER TWELVE

**AT LUNCHTIME SHERRI WENT BACK TO TONY'S LUNCHEONETTE.**

Tony greeted her warmly. "Hey there, Sherri!" he called, beaming from behind the counter. "Back again, huh? Are you going to eat this time, or are you still hunting for Ben?"

"I saw him at the high school. I'm here for lunch."

"Grab a seat, kid. I'll be right with you."

"Thanks."

As Sherri approached the counter, a woman turned on her stool to face her. It was Paula, the woman she had met on the road—the one Mac called a conspiracy theorist. She wore tattered jeans and a faded David Bowie concert T-shirt.

"Hey there, reporter girl. You want a story? I've got a story for you. It's called 'Shopwells Strikes Again: Paula Simcoe, Latest Victim.'" Grimacing, she patted the stool next to her.

Sherri slumped down. "What happened?"

"Same thing they did to Anita at the bookstore and to everyone else. I'm out of my record shop. Effective tomorrow."

"Can they do that?" Sherri asked. "I mean, doesn't your landlord have to give you notice? What about your lease?"

"My landlord sold to Shopwells. And they want me out. Sent a guy in a pricey suit to serve me the papers this morning."

"Can't you fight it?"

Paula snorted. "Yeah, right—me versus Shopwells' army of corporate lawyers. How do you think *that's* going to turn out?"

Tony leaned right up against the counter. "How about today's special."

"Sorry, Tony," Sherri said. "But if your special is anything like what they're serving at Shopwells, I think I'll stick with the menu."

Tony gave her a look. "Please, I've seen that garbage they serve. All my food is freshly prepared. No frozen junk here. The special today is a salmon burger and a garden salad for $5.95."

"Sounds great."

"Make that two," Paula said, and Tony disappeared into the kitchen. "What's all this about the food at Shopwells?"

Sherri lowered her voice. "Paula, it's not just about Shopwells putting everyone in town out of business. They're doing something to the people who work there—I know it. And I think it has something to do with the food they serve." Quickly, she filled Paula in on what happened between Tom Willard and PK Peterson, as well as Uncle Walter's strange behaviour after eating the staff special. "What do you think?" Sherri asked as Tony placed their food on the counter.

"I wouldn't put anything past that damn place," Paula said. "You're onto something."

The bell over the front door jangled and Paula turned. Her eyes narrowed.

"Speak of the devil." Sherri followed her gaze and saw Rebecca step into the luncheonette.

"Or the devil's handmaiden."

Rebecca walked right up to the two of them. She wore the same dark, square-cut suit and black pumps as before. Sherri wondered if that was a requirement of Shopwells'. She pictured a closet full of identical black pencil skirts and high-necked white blouses.

"Here comes Lewton's star reporter to eat among the common folk," Paula said, turning her back on Rebecca. "Oh, my mistake, you're not a reporter anymore. You're a sellout."

"Paula, don't be like this," Rebecca said in a gentle voice.

"I've got nothing to say to you." Paula looked mad enough to spit.

Sherri looked from one woman to the other.

"Come on, Paula," Rebecca said. "Are you really going to blame one person working at one store for all of your troubles?"

"Yes, I am." Paula whirled to face Rebecca. "And you don't know shit about my problems, lady."

"I heard the news."

"Gee, I wonder how you heard the news."

"I'm sorry," Rebecca said as if Paula hadn't spoken. "I know your store means a lot to you and, while I know it wouldn't be the same, I've come to offer you an alternative. You'd make a great manager of our music and electronics department."

Paula let go a jagged, bitter laugh. "Are you out of your mind, lady? I'd rather end up begging on the street with an old coffee cup than work at Shopwells. And you, you're part of the problem! You went over to the dark side."

"This isn't a science fiction movie, Paula," Rebecca said. "I'm just one person doing her job."

"One person, huh? So that's your line? What difference does one person make?" Paula accentuated her words with sharp jabs to Rebecca's shoulder. "Let me tell you, it *all* makes a difference. Shopwells is putting every store in Lewton out of business, one at a time." Paula dug into her pocket and tossed a ten-dollar bill on the counter. "Keep the change, Tony. I've lost my appetite. I'm outta here."

"I'll come with you," Rebecca said. "I know you're upset right now, but you really need to hear about the job we're offering you."

As Paula pushed past, Sherri reached out and grabbed Rebecca's arm. "Not so fast," Sherri said. "What were you talking to my uncle about on the phone last night?"

"I was following up with him about getting the Mini fixed," Rebecca said without missing a beat.

"At ten o'clock at night?"

"What's this all about, Sherri?"

"This is all about how my Uncle Walter has become a zombie since he started working at your store and why the hell I walked out of that place with bags full of crap I'll never use."

Rebecca stared at her.

"And what about Shopwells buying out all the businesses in town?"

"That's quite the imagination you have, Sherri. Maybe instead of being a reporter, you should write fiction?"

"I don't think so. I know there's a story here and so do you. You were covering it once."

Rebecca stiffened. They stared at each other for a moment.

"Please help me, Rebecca. I'll never reveal my source."

"I thought Mac warned you. Try something like this again, and your little summer internship is over."

She turned and left.

Tony came out of the kitchen drying his hands on his apron. "You have to watch out for that one," he said. "She was real nice when she first got here."

"What changed her?" Sherri asked, watching Rebecca disappear down the street.

"Shopwells. It changes everyone." He picked up Paula's abandoned plate. "You'll like the salmon burger."

"Mmm." Sherri took a bite. "Delicious."

"Stop by for breakfast tomorrow and I'll whip you up a stack of my famous buttermilk pancakes. Ben'll be here."

Viv smiled up at Sherri from her desk when Sherri walked back into the office after lunch.

"Hey, Viv. Can I get the key to the morgue?"

Viv's smile faltered. "Krystal doesn't like people rifling around up there. Maybe you should ask her to find what you want?"

"I'll just pop in and out. She won't even know I've been in there."

"Well all right," Viv said, retrieving a silver key tied onto a piece of fraying twine. "But if she sees you, don't tell her I gave it to you. Tell her you grabbed it off my desk when I was at lunch. I don't need the hassle."

"You got it." Sherri grabbed the key.

At the top of the stairs, she paused in the empty corridor and listened. Krystal's office door was shut, and the sound of her talking on the phone filtered into the hallway. Mac's desk stood empty. Silently, Sherri unlocked the door to the morgue and slipped inside.

The morgue was dark, dank and smelled of dust. Sherri stifled a sneeze and groped at the wall for a light switch. A naked bulb shone overhead. Plain wooden shelves lined the walls, and each ledge was tagged with old-fashioned labels with dates. Above them sat stacks of *The Lewton Leader-Post*. Sherri scanned the labels.

The papers, faded to a sallow yellow, went back a full calendar year. The front page of the oldest was dated June of the year before. Sherri reached for it. If Rebecca had been on the job for a year and had covered Shopwells from the beginning, then her stories had to be here. Sherri was surprised to find a giant announcement on page two. It read:

### LEADER-POST WELCOMES NEW REPORTER.

Rebecca Scott, 25, is excited to join the paper as the new municipal reporter. She comes with a journalism degree from Queen's University.

Sherri felt a twinge of envy. She moved on to the next edition. The front page featured a story about the week's council meeting with Rebecca's byline. Sherri's eyes scanned the page, but all she found was an article about new uniforms for the town's three-person fire department and an upcoming tender for snow removal services. Then, bingo! Her eyes fell on the last sentence:

Next week: council will debate the new Shopwells Super Centre proposed for lot 1428 Elm Street, on the north edge of town.

Sherri folded the paper quickly and went for the next edition.

But the front page of the next week's edition had no story about the council meeting. Neither did page two or three. Nothing. Sherri flipped through the entire edition, but the story Rebecca had promised the week before wasn't there. Sherri glanced back to the front page and noticed the date on the paper was correct—the last week of June—but the year was wrong. It was a whole year *earlier* than the previous edition.

The shelf held several copies of the same edition. Sherri flipped through them all, but they were all the same. *Last year's papers are all missing.* Only when she reached March did last year's editions reappear—in time for Krystal's first byline as the new municipal reporter. Rebecca must have left to join Shopwells in the first week of March.

Sherri slumped against a shelf. Her fingers were stained black with newsprint and her mind whirled as she tried to figure out her next step.

Suddenly the door groaned open and Krystal stood there, glaring.

"What are you doing in here?"

"Nuclear fission," Sherri quipped, moving to slide a sheet out from the paper that lay open in front of her. "You ruined hours of careful scientific experiments. Shame on you." Sherri moved to push past her, but Krystal blocked her way.

"You're not supposed to be in here. What do you have there?" Krystal reached forward and snatched the page from Sherri's hand. She looked from the paper to Sherri and back again, looking confused and a little disappointed. "Why are you taking a story about last year's church bingo social?"

"Research," Sherri said. "I figure if I don't make the big

time as a community reporter, I can always make a living as a bingo shark." She plucked the page back from Krystal.

"Hmpf . . ." Krystal said, hovering behind Sherri as she stepped back into the hall. "Be sure you report to Viv what you've taken. We can't let this place go all to sixes and sevens."

"Sure thing," Sherri said, re-locking the door. "No sixes. No sevens. I'll even steer clear of eights. Although we might want to have a chat with Viv about this place," Sherri said, dusting off the knees of her pants.

"Why?" Krystal asked, her eyes narrowing.

"Well it looks like there are missing papers. A lot of them. There are hardly any of last year's editions."

"And why would you think Viv would get rid of papers?" Krystal asked.

*Wow,* Sherri thought, *you've got to be the worst liar in the world.* "I don't know," Sherri said. "Why do *you* think?" The two of them locked eyes.

Krystal held out her hand. "I'll take the key back down to Viv and tell her about the missing papers."

Reluctantly, Sherri put the key in Krystal's palm. "I'm sure you will," she muttered.

Back in her office with the door closed, Sherri fell into her chair, feeling trapped. *What next?*

She reached for a tissue from the box on her desk to wipe the ink off her hands before she smeared it all over the keyboard.

*The computer! Rebecca must have left some files on it!*

Surely Rebecca would have left stories and drafts behind when she went to work at Shopwells? And Sherri hoped that neither Mac nor Krystal, who both looked like they would be more comfortable on a rickety old Underwood typewriter, had wiped the hard drive clean.

Sherri shook her head as she switched on the computer. Why hadn't she thought about it having a history? Her computer now—but Rebecca's before. As she searched each folder, her enthusiasm waned until, in a last ditch effort, she used the search engine to locate all the Rebecca Scott files in the system. The computer buzzed and whirred and gave a terse beep: zero documents.

Someone knocked on the door and Mac peered in.

"I thought I gave you the afternoon off?"

"You did," Sherri said, forcing a smile. "But there's no internet at my aunt and uncle's, and I wanted to send a few emails if that's all right."

"Sure, no problem." Mac opened the door wider. "You look a little flushed. Might want to keep this open. No air circulation in here once the door is closed. Krystal was always complaining about it when this was her office."

*Of course! This used to be Krystal's office, and Krystal's in Rebecca's old office now!*

"Damn," Sherri muttered under her breath.

"What is it?"

"Nothing. Thanks for the tip, Mac. About the door, I mean."


At four o'clock, Krystal emerged from her office and announced loudly that she was off to a Committee of the Whole meeting, making it sound more like she was going to an exclusive one-on-one interview with the prime minister.

"Have fun," Sherri called, watching her go. Sherri moved to the window and watched Krystal climb into her beat-up Buick and disappear down the road.

"Mac," Sherri said, popping her head into his office, "how long does a Committee of the Whole meeting usually last?"

He shrugged. "A couple of hours. Why?"

She smiled sweetly. "Just curious."

# CHAPTER THIRTEEN

AT 5:15, KRYSTAL'S BUICK STILL HADN'T RETURNED. FINALLY, Sherri heard Mac close his office door. "Well that's it for another week," he said. "Paper's gone to bed. How does it feel, Richmond? Your first press day."

"Very exciting," Sherri said, fighting the urge to rush him out the door.

"Heading home now?" he asked.

"In a minute. Just a couple more things to take care of."

Mac nodded and put on his windbreaker. "Good night."

"Night."

After Mac's steps had died away, Sherri went to the window and watched him saunter down Main Street. Then she hurried into Krystal's office and sat down behind her desk. Krystal hadn't shut down the computer before she'd left for her meeting. A simple tap on the mouse and her messy desktop appeared, a haphazard collection of files, downloads and documents. *No password.* Sherri smiled. If Krystal didn't know her way around a computer, what were the chances she'd found Rebecca's files and deleted them?

If Mac was right, she had another forty-five minutes before Krystal would be back. Sherri began to dig, deeper and deeper. She went through the hard drive, checking each folder. Finally, she found one marked *RS*, buried three layers down.

"Hello, Rebecca," Sherri whispered and clicked on it. The *RS* folder was a picture of order; inside were other folders labelled by date. Each one held a handful of stories. Sherri opened the most recent folder and clicked on the first story.

### COUNCIL VOTES TO INCREASE
### PARKING FEES ON MAIN STREET.

Not too thrilling. But Sherri read through the story anyway. It was a draft that hadn't been to the copy editor. A few words were misspelled, and it had a couple of awkward sentences that could have used a rewrite. It looked like Rebecca didn't even know the difference between *they're* and *their. Ha!*

Sherri clicked on the next file when tires screeched outside the window. She froze. *Krystal and her ugly Buick are back. It's only five thirty!* Then she heard the slam of Krystal's car door.

Sherri ran to her office, grabbed a memory stick and dashed back. She shoved the stick into Krystal's computer and dragged all of Rebecca's files over. Then she closed all the windows on the desktop and straightened the things on Krystal's desk.

Sherri's heart thudded as she heard the front door open and close, followed by steps on the staircase. She heard the familiar groan of the floorboards outside Mac's office. Sherri leapt out of Krystal's chair and bolted from the room. Krystal was too close for her to get back to her own office, so Sherri stopped in front of the hallway printer, smacked its side and swore. "Goddamn thing!"

"Sherri?" Krystal was wrapped in a faded denim jacket complete with rhinestones on the collar. She clutched a notebook to her chest.

"The one and only," Sherri said, not taking her eyes away from the printer. She gave it another smack for good measure. She felt Krystal's eyes on her.

"Why are you here?" Krystal asked.

"I work here, remember?"

"It's way past five."

"I have to get my notes printed for tomorrow," Sherri said, feigning a grimace. "And I'm in a battle to the death with the printer."

Krystal smirked, her look implying that Sherri was about on par with a monkey when it came to understanding complex office equipment. "Is there an emergency bake sale tomorrow that I haven't heard about?"

Sherri gritted her teeth. Only the knowledge that she had pillaged Krystal's computer kept her from smacking the woman. "You should think about getting into stand-up, Krystal," Sherri said, turning to her office. "You are oh so funny."

"Well *I'm* back from the Committee of the Whole," Krystal said as if it were something to be proud of. "There was an important meeting about new park benches that I'm sure will take up most of next week's front page."

"Thrilling," Sherri said as she plunked down at her desk. "If you don't mind, Krystal, I'd like to get out of here sometime tonight." She opened her email, ignoring Krystal. There was one from Michael, but she didn't have the patience to read it just now. Krystal harrumphed and went to her own office. Sherri held her breath, wondering if Krystal had noticed something amiss with her computer. Silence. Then came the familiar, hesitant hunt-and-peck sound of Krystal's typing.

Sherri plugged in the memory stick and did a search for the word "Shopwells." Twenty documents popped up. Sherri opened the files and printed them all, along with Michael's email. Out in the hallway, the printer whirred to life.

The sound of Krystal's typing stopped. "Printer seems to be working fine now," she called.

Sherri hurried to the printer. "Those are mine," she called out. Krystal was already there, hovering, poised to strike.

Sherri swooped in, grabbing the pages. *Let's see if you've got the nerve to take them right out of my hands.* But Krystal didn't move.

"Seems sort of long for interview notes," Krystal said. "Who did you say it was with?"

"I didn't. Normally I would have taped the interview, but I've been having issues with my recorder ever since you took the batteries out," Sherri shot back.

"Don't you know anything about being a reporter, Sherri? You have to check your facts before you make accusations; otherwise you could get into a lot of trouble."

As Sherri turned to go back to her office, the printer spat out a single page.

Krystal reached out and plucked it from the machine before it was free from the spindle.

*Oh shit!* Sherri thought.

Krystal glanced at the page, then up at Sherri, then back

down at the page. A condescending smile twisted up the corners of her mouth. "It may be after hours, Sherri, but you shouldn't be using office equipment to print personal things." Krystal handed her the page.

"I'll keep that in mind," Sherri said.

She glanced down and saw it was the email from Michael, with his familiar abbreviations.

> Sher:
>
> Did u get my voicemail? Pls call me back. I told u I wont see Anna anymore, k? Luv u. M

Sherri turned to go.

"Looks like there's trouble in paradise you might want to attend to," Krystal called after her.

Sherri wasn't about to let the dig get to her. Not when she was clutching the stack of Rebecca's stories to her chest. On her way out of the office, she dropped Michael's email in the recycle bin.

Sitting cross-legged on her bed in the lavender room, Sherri spread the printouts of Rebecca's stories across the flowered coverlet. She arranged them by date, then read from the beginning.

First there was a story about the Town Council meeting which had approved the Shopwells application to build. Another story was about a group of townspeople led by Paula Simcoe, protesting outside the town hall. After that came updates on the construction. A couple of new zoning amendments had been passed to give the store a much bigger footprint. Sherri was surprised at the critical tone of Rebecca's reporting. How could that stern young woman in the severe skirts and high-necked blouses be the same person who had written these?

The stories covered details that Sherri more or less already knew. *Why would Krystal bother pulling these stories from the morgue?*

But one story stood out. It was toward the end of Rebecca's time at the paper. It was an interview with Tom Willard when he still had his hardware store.

> Mr. Willard says he fears for his livelihood once the big box store opens its doors next month. He alleges that a representative from the Shopwells Corporation approached him about buying the building and land that currently houses Willard's Home Solutions. Representatives from Shopwells did not return calls for comment.

And then, in the next week's edition, a bizarre follow-up:

> The latest high profile recruit to Shopwells management staff is Tom Willard. Commenting on behalf of Willard, Shopwells head office issued a statement saying the company is happy to have an experienced local businessman join their team.

An note at the bottom of the draft sent Sherri's reporter radar off the charts. It was a message from Rebecca to Mac.

*** Mac: I'm headed to Shopwells after I file today to try and get a hold of Tom and find out why the sudden switcheroo. I wonder if this is the start of a strategy to rope in our downtown business people. If so, this is big. Don't worry, I'll play hardball. I'll get the story. RS

Sherri looked at the date. March 11. Rebecca's last week at the paper.

She fell back onto her bed and exhaled. Her mind swirled. It was the interview with Tom Willard that Rebecca never came back from, Sherri guessed. Or not Rebecca the reporter, anyway. By the next week, her byline had disappeared from the paper, and Rebecca was the new PR girl at Shopwells.

*What turned a solid reporter like her into a corporate lapdog? I have to get Tom to talk.*

The bedroom door creaked open. Uncle Walter peered in. He wore his orange Shopwells vest. The sight of it gave Sherri a chill.

"What have you got there, dear?"

"Just some stuff for work." She quickly gathered up the papers and shoved them into the drawer of the night table.

"Good for you. Don't put off until tomorrow what you can do today; that's number four on Shopwells' Top Ten Credos for a Successful Employee."

"Uh, great," Sherri said. "I can't wait to hear the other nine."

"Oh, well I'll get you a copy of them. You can keep it posted on your desk."

"Right, I'll do that. Was there something you wanted, Uncle Walter?"

"Your Aunt Gillian sent me up to tell you that dinner will be ready in five minutes. Meat pie. It used to be one of my favourites. You'll love it."

"Great. See you in the dining room."

"Righty-o," he said, heading downstairs.

Sherri slipped into the bathroom to wash up. When she stepped back into the bedroom a few minutes later, she noticed the night table drawer was slightly open. She rushed over to it. The stories were gone.

Sherri bounded down the stairs and into the kitchen where Aunt Gillian was already dishing out giant portions of meat pie.

"Just in time, dear. Take a seat."

"Where's Uncle Walter?"

"Oh, you know, he's off to Shopwells for the evening shift."

# CHAPTER FOURTEEN

IT WAS JUST AFTER 8:00 A.M. EARLY WAS PERFECT. TOM WILLARD was sure to be home and awake, ready to head off to work. Sherri would corner him, charm him and get him to trust her. He would finally talk.

Tom's blue two-storey house surprised Sherri. It looked nothing like the rundown weather-beaten houses she drove past along the bumpy country road, east of downtown. While the other houses had peeling paint and weathered facades, Willard's house looked neat and tidy in the early morning sunlight, with fresh paint on the shutters and a well-tended garden of yellow impatiens in full bloom.

With her reporter's notebook tucked under her arm and the recorder in her pocket, complete with fresh batteries, Sherri stepped up onto the narrow porch and rang the bell. A dog barked, but no one came to the door. Sherri knocked and waited. No sound of footsteps from within. No voices. She peered through the narrow window running alongside the front door and looked inside. There was the flicker of a shadow, a movement, in the back. But no one came to the door. Sherri knocked again.

"Mr. Willard?" she called through the glass. "It's Sherri Richmond from the paper. I'd like to speak with you."

Around the side of the house was a large window about five feet off the ground. Sherri dragged a nearby recycling bin over, tipped it upside down and climbed on top to peer inside. The window looked into the kitchen. Plump, iridescent green houseflies buzzed around the table, where a half-chopped banana, with skin beginning to brown, lay next to a bowl of breakfast cereal. A chair had been pushed back, as if someone had stepped away for a moment and forgotten to come back for the food.

Past the kitchen was a dim sitting room with the blinds drawn. Snowy static played on the television screen, bathing the couch and two chairs in an eerie glow. Nothing moved.

Suddenly, a German shepherd that looked the size of a horse jumped at the window, barking and snapping. Its breath fogged the glass and flecks of foam clung to its yellow teeth. Sherri yelled and tottered backward. She jumped off the recycling bin, pulled out her cellphone and dialled Tom's home number. The line rang, but the phone inside the kitchen did not.

The number you have dialled is no longer in service. Please check the number and dial your call again.

Sherri dialled Shopwells.

Thank you for shopping well at Shopwells. For service in English, press one.

Sherri hit one.

> Thank you for shopping well at Shopwells. For store hours and location, press one. For our electronics department, press two. For our automotive department, press three.

It went on and on with numbers for every department.

> To repeat these options, press the pound key. To speak with an operator, press zero. If you know your party's four-digit extension, you may enter it now. To dial by last name, press the star key.

Sherry hit the star key and typed in "Willard."

> We're sorry. We don't have a listing for that name. Thank you for shopping well at Shopwells. For store hours and location, press one.

Fuming, Sherri hit zero to speak to an operator.

> Thank you for shopping well at Shopwells. Our store is now closed. Please call back during regular business hours.

"Shit!" Sherri jumped in her car and headed for Shopwells.

Only a handful of cars were parked in the Shopwells lot when Sherri screeched to a halt by the front doors. She stepped out and made a beeline for the entrance. But a long line of shopping carts blocked her path.

A familiar voice said, "Sorry about that, I just have to get these carts inside before we open."

It was Anita from the bookshop. She wore a placid, half-asleep smile and showed no spark of recognition. The giant nametag pinned to her orange vest read: ANITA, BOOK DEPARTMENT SUPERVISOR.

"Anita?" Sherri said, walking up to her.

Anita blinked.

"It's me, Sherri." She stopped herself before adding "from the paper" for fear it would set off a secret alarm. "We met the other day at the bookshop, remember? You were going to find me a copy of *Jane Eyre*."

Anita cocked her head and blinked again. It reminded Sherri of a dog trying to puzzle out its master's command.

"Can I help you with something?" Anita asked.

"I have to speak to the assistant manager. Can you take me to him?"

"I'd be pleased to help you with anything you need as soon as we open."

"Thanks, but it's really Tom Willard I need to speak with."

"Just a moment, please. Let me take these carts inside, and I'll see what I can do for you. Wait right here." Anita walked up to the front doors, where a security guard let her in before locking up behind her again.

Sherri waited.

After several minutes, a towering security guard in a black

uniform stepped out of the store and marched up to Sherri.

"I'm sorry, Miss Richmond, but I'm going to have to ask you to leave."

"What for?"

"You're not permitted on Shopwells property. I have explicit instructions from management."

"Funny, it's management I'm here to see. I need to speak to Tom Willard."

The guard's expression didn't change. "Leave now or I'll call the police."

Sherri tried to push past him, but the guard grabbed her arm, turned her around and marched her back toward the Mini. "Get your hands off me!" she yelled.

"You will be charged with trespassing. You must leave now."

"I'm going, I'm going! But tell your PR lackey that manhandling customers doesn't make for good press! I'll be back."

The guard stood next to her car with his arms folded across his chest until she got in and drove away.


It was after 9:00 a.m. when Sherri pulled up in front of Tony's Luncheonette. For a moment she felt as though her breath had been knocked out of her. She stared for what seemed like an eternity.

Then she leapt out of the car and ran over to the papered-over windows of the luncheonette. A lone car rumbled behind her on Main Street. Sherri stood staring at the pasted Shopwells flyers. She tried the front door. Locked.

"Tony?" she called through the glass. "Tony!" She banged her fist against the door until the glass rattled. "Hello?" She waited for the sound of steps approaching, for the sound of the lock turning. She pictured Tony and Ben inside, packing up cardboard boxes full of chipped dishes and stained coffee mugs. Maybe in a moment Ben would appear at the door, looking tired and sad, but then his face would light up when he saw her.

But nothing stirred.

Sherri turned and ran through the narrow brick alley between Tony's and the closed sewing shop next door. She almost tripped over an overturned garbage can, but regained her balance and kept going. Around the back, a lone wooden door with a glass window led to the luncheonette's kitchen. A yellowing Shopwells flyer advertising ladies' lace gloves covered the window. Sherri banged at it with a closed fist.

"Is anyone in there? It's Sherri!" Silence.

She tried the handle and was surprised when the door opened. Inside the dark kitchen, only the faint outline of the fridge was visible. The low hum of its motor seemed to amplify the tick tock of the kitchen clock.

"Tony?" Sherri took a cautious step in and reached for the wall, feeling for the light switch. The kitchen suddenly buzzed to life, and Sherri squinted against the harsh fluorescent lights as the overhead fan groaned awake, making slow creaky circles. Nothing else stirred. Somehow, this felt worse.

In the dark, the diner only seemed to be closed, as if it were after hours and everyone had gone home. But now, with the lights on in a kitchen that should have been bustling with breakfast orders, the full impact of the situation hit Sherri. She went through the swinging door to the dining area, where she had sat at the counter with Paula yesterday.

"Tony?" she called again, not really expecting him to answer, but hoping for the sound of something, anything, to fill up the emptiness of the place. Up front, the papers covering the front windows made it feel like night. A small stack of yellowed flyers and a roll of masking tape lay on a table close to the windows. A plate of cold food was still on the counter—a half-eaten hamburger and a few crinkle-cut fries next to a lump of flaky dry ketchup. A fly circled and landed on the cold meal. An abandoned glass of soda had a red lipstick mark on its rim. The whole scene looked just like Tom Willard's breakfast table.

Ducking into the kitchen, Sherri opened the double doors of the creaky old refrigerator. The shelves sagged with fresh food: crisp heads of lettuce, bright red tomatoes, dozens of eggs and packets of ground beef.

It was a restaurant ready to open for business.

*So where the hell is Tony?*

But more importantly, where was Ben?


**M**ac! Mac!" Sherri nearly stumbled taking the front stairs two at a time. When she got to Mac's door, she found him sitting at his desk, smiling.

"Hold on a sec, Richmond," he said, holding up his hand. "Take a look at this." He tossed a copy of the paper across the desk to her. "I remember *my* first byline in a real paper," he said, sounding wistful. "Now I know you've been all over your school paper. But this is different."

The headline at the top of the page was on a Committee of Adjustment debate about a tax increase. But there, below the crease that separated the paper in two, was Sherri's giant full-colour photo of Ben, beneath a blaring headline:

## Local Bands Battle for Glory
### by Sherri Richmond, Community Reporter.

"You put it on the front page!" Sherri said, trying not to sound too awed.

Mac shrugged. "It's a good story. I told you." He smiled. "I'm sure your friend will be pleased. But if I get any complaints about not putting the winning band up front, I'm bunting the calls to you. Deal?"

"Deal. But you have to come with me right now."

"What is it?"

"Tony's gone! His place is shut down, but it's *not*. It looks as if he disappeared in the middle of cleaning up after a customer."

Mac jolted at the mention of Tony's, but then he seemed to calm down.

"Richmond," he sighed. "I thought you understood my position on this whole thing. This is not a story for *The Lewton Leader-Post*."

"But what about Ben and Tony? They're gone!"

"They're not *gone*, Richmond. They're just not at work. I'm sure they'll turn up somewhere."

"Yeah, at Shopwells, just like everyone else!"

"Sherri, sit down."

Reluctantly, Sherri sat.

"I'm looking out for you here. I want you to do well. So I'd like you to cover some events in one of our northern communities called Sunridge. You'll be out of town overnight, maybe two nights. I'll book you into the Sunridge Hotel. See Viv before you leave and she'll set you up with some petty cash to cover your gas and meals."

"What's the big assignment in Sunridge?"

"There's a community dance tonight with a live band."

"Am I your music correspondent now?"

"Sunridge is an important area for us. It's only about an hour north, but they don't have a paper of their own and a lot of their businesses advertise with us in the summer to get the tourists up there." He tossed a folder to her across the desk. "Here are the details of your assignment. Tonight there's the dance, tomorrow there's a charity euchre tournament in the afternoon and a strawberry social after that. It's all outlined here. You'll get a full two-page spread special in next week's edition. It'll look very impressive in your portfolio."

Sherri stared down at the folder, trying to resist the urge to toss it back. But she tucked it under her arm, feeling exhausted and frustrated.

She got up to go.

"Sherri," Mac called after her. "It's too bad. About Tony's, I mean."

# CHAPTER FIFTEEN

PACKING WAS IMPOSSIBLE. DISTRACTED, SHERRI SHOVED CLOTHES randomly into her overnight bag. One minute she was folding a T-shirt and glancing at the list from Mac's folder, the next she was pulling clothes out again, determined to stay.

"Pick up the goddamn phone, Ben." She dialled Ben's cellphone over and over. She kept picturing him glassy-eyed, in an orange vest, handing out flyers for this week's special on gardening gloves.

Sherri was stuffing a green dress into her bag for the third time when she heard footsteps creaking on the floor below.

Aunt Gillian called from the landing: "Sherri? There's someone here to see you, dear."

Sherri froze. "I'll be right there, Aunt Gillian." *Who is it?* Sherri inched her way to the window and peered out from behind the curtain. A car was in the parking lot next to the Mini, but it was half-obscured by the giant willow. *Could it be Mac?* No, he would call her if he wanted to speak to her. Then she imagined Rebecca standing in the kitchen, waiting for her. She would put on the same fake smile that she had at Tony's— right before Tony disappeared and his place shut down.

"Sherri? We're waiting," Aunt Gillian called again.

"Be right there."

But when she peered tentatively into the kitchen, she noticed a head of familiar, sandy red hair.

"Ben!" Sherri flung her arms around his neck. Ben stumbled backward, startled, and tipped over a jar of Aunt Gillian's pepper raspberry jam.

"My goodness!" Aunt Gillian gasped.

"Guess I should drop in more often, huh?" Ben joked.

"Sherri?" Aunt Gillian said, her hand on her chest. "Is everything all right?"

"Everything's fine," Sherri said, pulling away from Ben to look up at his face. His green eyes still sparkled and he had the same boyish smile. Yes, it was the same Ben. "Aunt Gillian, this is—"

"Oh, I know the young man, Sherri."

"Small town, remember?" Ben said, placing the jar of jam back on the shelf.

"We'll be in the living room, Aunt Gillian." Sherri led Ben out of the kitchen.

"I'll bring you out some snacks. Benjamin, you let me know if you'd like a jar of that jam. It's lovely on toast."

"Thanks, Mrs. Richmond," Ben said as he followed Sherri out.

"Jesus, Ben," Sherri said, lowering her voice and gesturing for him to sit. "I was trying to get you on your phone all day. What happened?"

"Sorry," Ben said, as he sank into the faded old couch. "I haven't really been in a talking mood. I worked for Tony forever."

"So what happened?" Sherri said. "When I saw that it had

closed down, I thought the worst."

"I woke up this morning for my shift and there was only this." Ben pulled out his cellphone, tapped a few buttons and showed Sherri the display screen:

> Ben, don't bother coming in this a.m. Sorry, but I've closed the luncheonette. We'll square up for your last shift soon. T.

"Funny," Ben said as Sherri read the text, "that when the guy finally gets the hang of texting it's to sack me."

"No way Tony wrote this."

"Who then?"

Sherri put a finger to her lips as Aunt Gillian swept into the room with a tray of Ritz crackers topped with five different kinds of jam and two giant glasses of milk.

"Here you go! Sherri, fill up before you hit the road," Aunt Gillian said. She hovered until Sherri took a buttery cracker and popped it into her mouth.

"Mmmm," Sherri said, giving her the thumbs up. "Thanks, Aunt Gillian."

"Yeah, thanks," Ben said. They didn't say anything else until Aunt Gillian, placated, returned to the kitchen.

"Why do we have to be quiet when your aunt's in the room?" Ben asked. "You think she's in on all this? C'mon."

"All I know is that my uncle works at Shopwells and you know what that means. The night before last, I heard him on the phone in the hallway—I know he was talking about me and he was talking to Rebecca. Then, last night, he stole a bunch of articles on Shopwells that I'd downloaded from Rebecca's old computer."

"He's spying on you for Shopwells? That's sick."

"That's what I was trying to tell you at the Battle of the Bands but, well . . ." She trailed off. It didn't feel like the right time to rehash their argument, not before she had a chance to show him today's paper.

"The thing is," Sherri said, lowering her voice to a whisper, "I don't think Uncle Walter *realizes* what he's doing. I don't think any of them do. Ben, I think it's the food."

Aunt Gillian appeared again, a giant smile on her face. "Can I get you two anything else?"

"We're fine, Aunt Gillian. Thanks."

"Are you sure? Oh, it's so nice to have a guest in the house again! Surely you'll both want some lunch?"

"I have to get going soon, Aunt Gillian, remember?"

"Oh, that's right," Aunt Gillian said, her face falling.

Sherri suddenly felt bad for taking away Aunt Gillian's first chance in ages to fuss about a guest. Her aunt retreated to the kitchen.

"I can't talk about it here," Sherri whispered to Ben. Maybe her aunt was listening in. "I don't know what she'll tell my uncle, even if she doesn't mean to."

"Why don't we go for a walk then?" Ben said.

"I have to hit the road." Sherri told him about her two-day banishment to Sunridge. "It's a long story." An idea suddenly struck her, and the words were out of her mouth before she could stop them. "Why don't you come with me? There's going to be a dance tonight." She blushed.

Ben looked surprised, then pleased. "Yeah," he said, nodding. "I guess I don't exactly have to report to work or anything, do I? Getting away would be nice. I'll drive—I know the way. And you'll fill me in on what's going on?"

"I'll tell you everything on the way," Sherri said.

"Okay," Ben said, getting to his feet. "Give me half an hour to dash home and pack a bag."

"No way," Sherri said, taking him by the wrist. "I'm not letting you out of my sight!"

"Aw, c'mon. What's the big deal?"

"Do you know where Tony is? Have you seen him since the luncheonette closed?"

"No."

"Well I saw Anita after her bookstore closed. Guess where?"

Ben's eyes widened. "And you think Tony might be . . .? No! No freaking way. Tony hates Shopwells with a fiery passion. He wouldn't be caught dead shopping, let alone *working* there."

"I'll bet you he's cooking up a batch of the staff special right now."

Ben took a breath. "Fine, I won't go home. I'm low maintenance. I'll manage. Oh, I almost forgot why I originally came by." From the back pocket of his jeans, Ben pulled out a folded newspaper clipping. It was the front page of *The Post*. "This is pretty awesome, Sherri. I wanted to say thanks."

"I felt like a real jerk about yesterday."

"Well if every time you feel like a jerk you decide to put me on the front page, that works for me."

Sherri laughed. "Come upstairs while I finish packing. We can stop at your house on the way."

They were halfway up the first flight of stairs when Aunt Gillian called to them.

"What was the name of that hotel where you'll be staying tonight, dear? I should have the number on hand just in case."

Sherri hesitated. *Now I'm just being paranoid.*

"It's the Sunridge Hotel, Aunt Gillian. I'll leave you the number."

The inside of Ben's beat-up Toyota Tercel smelled like old leather and Ben's cologne. A band Sherri had never heard before was playing on the radio as she got in.

"They're good," Sherri said, nodding to the beat.

"That's my demo," Ben said, smirking.

Sherri blushed. "You were right. When you hang together, you're really good."

"Thanks. Let's hit the road." The car rattled and rumbled as Ben turned the key. Aunt Gillian stood waving from the porch of the farmhouse as they pulled away.

Ben took less than five minutes to stop at his place. He emerged from the apartment with a small brown bag.

Barely five minutes into the drive, Ben flicked off the music. "We have officially passed the town limits."

"This place is smaller than I thought."

"And I don't see your aunt or uncle running after us in the rearview mirror. No one in an orange vest."

"*Not* funny," Sherri said.

"Spill it. What's going on?"

Sherri took a breath and, fully aware how crazy she might sound, she barrelled through the events of the past two days.

"And a couple of things are bugging me. That security guard at Shopwells knew my name. It was as if they were expecting me and that was right after my uncle took those stories from my desk. And Tom Willard's name isn't in the Shopwells directory. I tried to call him and there wasn't a listing. And when I went to his house it looked like he'd left in a hurry in the middle of breakfast, just like Tony. Tom even left his dog behind."

Ben gave her a look. "Tom doesn't have a dog. He's massively allergic. He sneezes just thinking about dogs."

"Well he's got a dog now! A huge German shepherd. The thing nearly broke through the window to get at my jugular."

"Well that's just freakin' weird."

"And there's also the food. My uncle only eats that glop, and he walks around like a zombie. I'll bet everyone in Shopwells lives off the staff special. I'm telling you, Ben, those people are being controlled."

"But if it's the food that's messing with people's heads, why were you affected? You said the first time you were in there you felt this urge to buy stuff. But you didn't eat the special, did you?"

"Damn. You're right. Maybe there's something else." Sherri thought about it for a minute. "I *did* have a drink at the cafeteria that first day when I met Rebecca. Maybe whatever's in the staff special is in *everything* they serve?"

"But then wouldn't the whole town be acting totally stoned? Everyone would have to be eating the staff special. But, well, it sounds like it's for the staff, right?"

"Are you helping or not?" Sherri asked, frustrated.

"Hey, I want to help! I'm just saying I think you need some proof about this staff special. I mean, did you get your hands on any? Test it?"

"You mean like with test tubes and a microscope? I'm not a scientist, Ben, I'm a reporter. I don't have a secret lab back at the farmhouse. I'm telling you, I *feel* it," she said, irked. But he was right. She *didn't* have any concrete proof. "I guess one of us could taste it, and we could see what happens."

"Excuse me? *One of us?* Sorry, Sherri. You're the reporter. If you want to sample the mind-altering food manufactured by a big bad mega corp, go for it. I'll observe your reaction and take notes."

"I thought you didn't believe me?" Sherri countered.

"I said you didn't have proof. But I'm not lining up to *be* your proof, sorry."

They drove in silence for a while. Then Ben signalled and turned off the highway.

"Are we there already?" Sherri asked.

"No, but I'm starving. There's a good burger place around here just up the way."

They sat at a picnic table in front of the roadside restaurant and ate burgers and fries from cardboard boxes.

Ben glanced at Sherri. "You okay?"

Sherri dabbed a french fry in ketchup but didn't eat it. "I can't believe I'm heading to the back of beyond for a community dance!" She slammed a fist against the table, frustrated.

"Hey, that's no way to behave on a first date."

Sherri smiled. "The date's not until the dance tonight."

"No, the date started when you got in my car. This is a good time for you to relax. You know you're onto something. But so do they. So we lie low for a while, right?"

"*Lie low?* Is this a gangster movie?"

"You know what I mean, Sherri," Ben said, shaking his head. "You do what Mac asked. You play nice. We go up north. You cover the little dance and the garage sale and the lemonade stand and whatever else. But when we get back—"

Sherri's cellphone rang and she dug in her purse for it.

"I bet it's your aunt," Ben said, teasing. "She's calling because you didn't pack enough jam and crackers."

"Oh, shut up," Sherri said, smiling. The call display read: *unknown number*. "Hello?" she said after flipping open the phone.

"This is Tom Willard."

Sherri's mouth dropped. She covered the mouthpiece and whispered to Ben: "It's Tom!"

"You wanted to talk to me," Tom said. "Well, now I'm ready to talk. Where can we meet?"

"Where are you?"

"It's better if you don't know."

"I went by your house this morning, and no one was there except for a big German shepherd."

"Those bastards."

"I tried to find you at Shopwells, but—"

"I don't work there anymore. Look, I can't talk about this on the phone. Where are you?"

"I'm on my way to Sunridge. Halfway there. I'm up there overnight on assignment."

"Where are you staying? I'll meet you there in a few hours."

# CHAPTER SIXTEEN

MOUNTED DEER HEADS, THEIR ANTLERS COVERED WITH COBWEBS, decorated the lobby of the Sunridge Hotel. The bald man behind the check-in counter fumbled with an old-fashioned guest register. He looked Sherri up and down, then turned his gaze on Ben.

"We've only got a reservation for one," the man said, tapping his pen on the open page of the register.

Ben shot Sherri a sideways glance. She smiled back.

"But the young lady's room does have a double bed."

Sherri felt her face burn beet red as she signed the book.

"I think maybe I should get my own room," Ben said in a low voice, pulling her aside.

"But then you'll have to pay."

Ben smiled. "I really like you, Sherri, and I'm glad that you invited me up here with you. But I think it's a good idea to go with two rooms."

Sherri looked up at Ben. *What a difference from Michael!* Then she gave him a hug.

"Wow." He laughed. "What would you do if I suggested separate hotels?"

Sherri playfully punched him on the shoulder and Ben turned back to the clerk.

"We'll take a second room, please," Ben said, handing him a credit card.

"Don't have anything ready right now," the clerk said, scanning his register. "Come back in a couple of hours, and I'll give you a key."

As Sherri and Ben walked toward the elevators, they passed a dingy bar off the lobby. It had flickering neon beer signs and a television with rabbit ears which was tuned to a baseball game. Sherri scanned the empty seats. There were no customers, only the bartender and a blonde waitress in a low-cut polka-dot dress, who absently polished a glass.

Inside the spartan room, Sherri tossed her bag onto the lumpy bed and stared out at the parking lot while Ben scoped out the bathroom. The room had faded orange shag carpeting and a flower-patterned bedspread of the same revolting hue. The framed photos of flowers on the wood-panelled walls were a faded greenish blue.

"Well, at least it's *clean*," Ben said with laughter in his voice. "And would you believe it's nicer than my little apartment in Lewton? Hey, you okay?"

Sherri paced back and forth. "Maybe we should wait here for Tom. Or in the lobby? Maybe we shouldn't even do the dance tonight. What if we miss him or he can't find us?"

"He'll call," Ben said, taking her by the shoulders. "Calm down. You're overthinking this. Tom'll find us. And you need to get your assignments done so everyone back in Lewton thinks you're being a good little reporter. We're going to the dance and we're going to have fun. Remember, this is still our date. Even if Tom is crashing it."

Sherri laughed and Ben leaned in, kissing her gently on the lips. It was fast, not at all what she had imagined their first kiss would be like. It was the first time Sherri admitted to herself that she had actually thought about their first kiss. Before it, she had still felt like Michael's girlfriend. But that was over now. She was with Ben.

"Why don't you get ready for the dance," Ben said. "I'll go down to the car and grab a proper shirt, so I don't disgrace you."

Ben reached for her hand as they walked to the dance. Sherri felt a rush of delight.

Sherri wore a white sweater over her green dress and the familiar heavy camera around her neck. She glanced at Ben out of the corner of her eye. He'd settled on a grey shirt, and in his free hand, he carried Sherri's bag with her camera equipment and notebook.

"We clean up pretty nice, don't we?" Ben said.

It seemed like every car in the tiny town was crammed into the gravel parking lot of the brown brick community centre. Outside, a string of red paper lanterns hung from the doorway. Folksy-rock music punctuated the evening air.

> *Outside the stars*
> *Are telling stories to each other*
> *Far above your bedroom window*
> *How I wish that I was up there . . .*

From around the corner of the community centre, Sherri caught the skunky smell of marijuana coming from a bunch of local kids. They looked uncomfortable in collared shirts and high heels.

Inside, Sherri checked in with an official-looking woman. She wore a tent-like pink dress and sat behind a card table, taking tickets. Sherri dropped her things in the corner and walked around the room. She snapped a great shot of an elderly couple dancing cheek to cheek with their eyes closed, and another of the lead singer up on the rickety stage belting into the microphone. Word spread quickly that a reporter from Lewton was in the crowd, and before long, the younger couples were gathering to pose for pictures. They crossed their eyes and made faces, but Sherri laughed and took the pictures anyway.

"I think you're done for the evening," Ben shouted over the music. He eased the camera from around her neck and tucked it under a table with Sherri's purse. He led her out onto the dance floor. But there was a big difference between Ben and the other men on the dance floor—he actually seemed to know what he was doing.

"You dance?" Sherri asked, trying to overcome her surprise and keep from trampling his toes.

"Oh sure," Ben said, swinging her along so that the full skirt of her green dress twirled. "I cook, I dance and I leap tall buildings in a single bound. There's a lot about me you don't know." He dipped her low and pulled her back up so that she pressed against his chest.

The band launched into a love song next. She rested her head on his shoulder and closed her eyes. They finished the dance without speaking. When the lead singer announced that the band would take a break, the crowd on the dance floor dispersed.

She felt suddenly nervous about Tom—he should have made it to Sunridge by now. Her eyes darted to the crowds that had begun to line up at the makeshift bar near the back of the hall.

"Did you want a drink?" Ben asked. He hadn't taken his palm away from the small of her back.

Sherri shook her head. "I was thinking we could call it a night. Head back to the hotel."

"Dying to be alone with me, huh?" He smiled.

"Yes I am." She gave him a quick kiss. "But I'm also dying to hear what Tom has to say."


The bald man wasn't sitting at the front desk when they returned to the hotel. Instead it was a young woman who looked barely older than Sherri. The woman, chewing gum, hardly glanced up from her copy of *People* magazine.

"Is my room ready? Last name's Quinlan," Ben asked.

She reached for a key and tossed it to Ben. "Here ya go. You're in 105."

"Excuse me," Sherri said "Did anyone leave a message for Sherri Richmond?"

The young woman nodded and gestured toward the bar. "He's in there," she said.

Sherri rushed into the bar. Tom sat in a corner beneath a giant retro movie poster for *The Body Snatcher*. The carpet felt sticky under her feet and the air smelled of stale beer.

"No minors!" the waitress barked at Sherri.

"S'all right," Tom Willard slurred, waving off the waitress, as Ben joined them. "This is my son and daughter come to see me. Hi kids!"

Sherri smelled the whiskey wafting off Tom as she sat down. Two chipped glass tumblers with little more than melting ice sat in front of him. In his hands, Tom cradled a third glass with a mouthful of rye left in it.

The waitress came with another drink.

"Get you kids a coke or somethin'?"

"No, thanks," Sherri said.

"Don't you count on getting another one of these," the waitress said to Tom as she gathered up the empty glasses. "We've got rules in this place, y'know."

"I'm not driving," Tom said handing her a twenty-dollar bill. The waitress pocketed the cash and left without a word.

Tom turned to Sherri. "I *wanted* to talk to you when you called the other night. I should've spoken to someone about this Shopwells stuff a long time ago. Last year, when Rebecca was doing your job, I almost told the story to her. She would have blown the whole thing wide open."

"Why didn't you?" Sherri pressed.

"I was all set to spill it to her, y'know. We were going to meet. I was nervous as hell. But then she showed up at the store—not to see me, not to talk, but *working* there! I thought she must be playing a joke on me. But there she was, wearing a suit and talking the company line. I got scared." He fidgeted with his glass, looking ashamed. "I figured if they could get to *her*, they could get to anyone."

"Tom, did Shopwells do something to you? Something to

persuade you to sell your store and go to work for them?"

"I was one of the first ones they got. The hardware store was losing money, and I knew it would lose even more once Shopwells opened up. They said they needed a good manager, someone who knew the town. I closed the store and took the job. But then they started." He took another drink.

Sherri felt her heart thud. She reached for her bag. "Let me get my recorder."

"No," Tom said, grabbing her wrist. "I don't want to be recorded and it can never get out that I was the one to tell you all this. If they knew it was me, that would be it."

"What would they do to you?" Ben asked.

Tom's eyes seemed to clear. "Plenty," he said. Then he swallowed another mouthful of whiskey.

*This has to be quick or he won't be in any condition to talk,* Sherri thought as she pulled out her notebook. "All right, tell me," she said with her pen poised. "Shopwells is doing something to the staff? Something you disagreed with, right? Is it the food?" she pressed. "Are they controlling people with the food?"

Sherri leaned in for the answer.

Tom looked at Sherri. "The *food?*"

"The staff special. I mean, it's like my uncle is addicted to that stuff. I haven't seen him eat anything else since I got to town. And after he eats it, he seems so out of it."

"The food is just a small part of the whole thing."

"Do they put something in the food?" Sherri asked.

"They tried it out in other locations first. It's supposed to be some kind of low protein crap that lowers resistance. They offer it free to the staff and, pretty soon, it's the only thing they're eating. Weakens the will."

"Crazy," Ben said.

"I knew it," Sherri said.

"But that wasn't enough for them. They decided to take things to the next level in Lewton. A small town seemed like the best place to test it out—seemed like the right place to get the employees under control. They tried out some things on the shoppers too."

"What?" Sherri asked.

"They brought in the music."

Everything snapped into place. "That's why I bought all that stuff I didn't need," Sherri said.

"Shopwells isn't the only big chain to do that, you know," Tom said. "Lots of stores do—they play music with subliminal messages. It's supposed to make customers buy stuff. Shopwells took it to the next level. Management has special earplugs to block out the frequency."

"And the workers?"

"Hold your horses, kid. I'm getting there. They *were* worried about how the music would affect the staff."

"Who?" Sherri demanded.

"Peterson," Tom said, spitting the name out. "He's the mastermind. This has been his baby from start to finish. He was the one who convinced head office to try it. I mean, how else do you get people to work minimum wage with no overtime, no health benefits, stocking shelves, and like it?"

"What was Peterson's big idea?"

"This," Tom said. He turned in his chair and tugged down the collar of his stained shirt. On the back of his neck, a couple of inches below his hairline, was an angry red scab.

"It looks like you were picking at a black fly bite," Ben said.

"It's not a bite," Tom said over his shoulder. "It's what they do to us, to all of us—like we're cats and dogs."

"What?" Sherri asked.

"Peterson says that he got the idea from vets. They inject cats and dogs with chips in case they get lost." He sounded sober for the first time that evening. "Damn, I wish I took it with me when I ran out of my house. But there was no time."

"Took what?"

"My chip," Tom said, lowering his voice. "It's how they control the workers. They implant a chip, and it sends a signal to the brain to make you nice and docile—little impulses to the brain. Makes you listen to everything they tell you and believe that losing your business and your home is okay, so long as you have a job at Shopwells."

"My God," Sherri said. "How do they control the chips?"

"The server's gotta be in Peterson's office."

"And you knew about this all the time?" Sherri asked.

"I didn't. Not at first. But when I asked too many questions, I got a chip of my own. They dragged me into the health clinic and injected me. I tried to fight them off. That was only yesterday."

A cold sick feeling twisted in Sherri's stomach as she pictured that sterile room down the long white hallway behind the warehouse at Shopwells—the room that Rebecca had said was a health clinic.

"So my Uncle Walter has one of those things in his neck, too?"

"All the workers do."

"What happened to yours?" Ben asked.

"I was lucky. I guess the technician didn't put it in deep enough. I was struggling. I knew it wasn't any damn flu shot they were trying to give me. Who gets a flu shot in the neck? Anyway, the tech's aim must have been off, because when I woke up this morning, the friggin' thing was on my pillow. Everything came back to me."

"What was it like with the chip?"

"Hard to describe. It's like you're walking through quicksand. Like you're in a dream. Part of you knows you're saying things that don't make sense, doing things you wouldn't do in a million years. I mean, why would I convince old lady Turlington to buy a push lawnmower? That woman can barely walk."

Just then the front door to the hotel slammed open like a gunshot and a man in black burst in. Instantly, Tom scrambled to his feet. "I've got to get out of here," he whispered.

But the man in black sauntered past the check-in counters and continued toward the elevators. Tom slumped back down. His hands trembled as he gripped his glass.

"You okay, Tom?" Sherri asked.

"Who else knows you're up here, aside from your editor?"

The realization hit her. *Oh, shit! My aunt and uncle.* "Um, no one," she lied.

Ben kicked her under the table, and Sherri gave him a look.

"Good," Tom said. "Alright, we've got to come up with something, fast."

"What's the plan?" Ben asked.

"I can sneak us into Shopwells," Tom said. "I've still got

my keys. Early tomorrow morning, say four o'clock. The cleaners won't have arrived yet, and the security guards will be changing shifts."

"What will we be looking for?" Sherri asked.

"Maybe another chip. I did some digging around on my own last week, when Peterson was out. I found some details about the chip program on his computer."

"How did you get into his computer?" Ben asked.

Tom laughed. "I guessed that idiot's password on the first go. He keeps a picture of his cat on his desk. Everyone knows its name. It's all he talks about. It's this giant white Persian that looks like it would kill you if you tried to pet it. *Lenny.* Didn't take a psychic to guess Peterson's password."

"Okay, then I'll be able to copy all the files off his computer." Sherri felt in her pocket for the memory stick she had used before. "Ben, you can search the health clinic and see if you can find the chips. Tom and I will sneak into Peterson's office. Agreed?"

Tom and Ben nodded.

"Good."

"I guess I'd better go sleep this off," Tom said, ambling to his feet. "Knock on my door at two o'clock. I'm in room 307."

# CHAPTER SEVENTEEN

**SHERRI AND BEN WATCHED TOM STAGGER OUT OF THE BAR.**

Ben shook his head. "This is so nuts. I don't know how I'm going to get any sleep." He stood up. "Come on. I'll walk you up."

"Oh," Sherri said. "But, what if I want to sleep in your room? It may be better than mine."

"Do you want to switch? We can do that."

"Maybe. But what if your room is *worse* than mine?"

Ben looked at her. "Hmm, yeah. That could be a problem."

"Well, there's only one way to find out. Let's go check out your room." She tilted her head up to kiss him, and they walked to room 105.

Ben opened the door.

"Yours is much nicer," Sherri said. The walls had been freshly painted and there were new hardwood floors. Sherri sat down on the queen-sized bed and bounced on the mattress. "This is so soft. I think the mattress in my room is stuffed with sawdust and nails."

"Okay, okay. You can totally have this room if you want," Ben said.

"That's sweet," Sherri said. "But maybe we could share after all."

"Yeah," he said, nodding, "we're probably not going to sleep much tonight as it is."

"Who needs sleep anyway?" Sherri said, pulling Ben down onto the bed.

The sound of smashing glass jolted Sherri awake. She lay still for a moment, breathing heavily, while Ben snored softly next to her with an arm across her waist.

*What time is it?* Sherri fumbled in the dark for the digital clock on the nightstand.

"Ben, wake up!" she said, jumping out of bed. She had already thrown on her clothes and was halfway out the door when Ben stirred. "What's going on?" he asked groggily.

"Get up. It's 2:15! I'll be right back. I've gotta let Tom know we're still coming." Sherri dashed up the back staircase to Room 307. The door gaped open.

"Tom?" she called, cautiously stepping inside. The drawers had been pulled out of the dressers and turned upside down. The sheets had been stripped from the bed to reveal the stained mattress, and the doors to the closet were wide open. Only wire hangers dangled there. The only sound in the room was the ominous tick tock of the alarm clock.

Sherri dashed down to Room 202. Her door was open too, and the room had been ransacked. The overnight bag that she'd left on the bed before the dance had been ripped open and her clothes littered the floor. Sherri shoved everything back into the bag and ran back downstairs. *Oh my God, please not Ben too!*

She pounded on his door. Ben answered it in his boxer

shorts. Sherri threw her arms around him.

"What's up?"

"Tom's gone. They grabbed him!"

"Calm down," Ben said as he pulled a shirt over his head and reached for his jeans. "Maybe he's out looking for some coffee or something?"

Sherri shook her head. "His room was empty and it's been torn apart. And so was mine. If we hadn't stayed down here last night, they would have got us too!"

"So what do we do now?" Ben asked.

"Finish getting dressed. We'll get a couple of my uncle's Shopwells vests and do this ourselves."


When Sherri and Ben pulled up to the entrance to Berry Grove, it was that silent early morning time—the crickets had stopped chirping and the birds hadn't yet begun to sing.

"Don't drive in," Sherri said. "I don't want to risk waking anyone." She undid her seatbelt. "I'll be right back."

"Don't want to introduce me to the family?" Ben joked. "Or was that just a one-night stand?"

"Plenty of time to meet the family, once we get through this."

In the pre-dawn light, Berry Grove seemed even creepier than usual. Sherri slipped through the front door and crept to the closet off the kitchen. Two of Uncle Walter's orange Shopwells vests hung there. *He must be on the early shift.* Sherri grabbed them and ducked out.

As she climbed back into the passenger seat, she tossed a vest to Ben. "Let's go!" Then she slipped hers on. "God, I feel dirty wearing this thing." She put her memory stick in one of the vest pockets.

"You're serious about this?" Ben asked, as he put the car into gear and steered toward Shopwells. "You think we can just waltz in there? This is a long shot without Tom."

"Haven't you seen any good zombie movies? All we have to do is look like them and walk like them. Then we've got a shot at getting in."

"And you don't think they're going to notice that it's you just because you're wearing an orange vest?"

Sherri shook her hair over her eyes. "Better?"

Sherri looked into Ben's face and realized he was frightened. Seeing that flicker of fear in his eyes made her notice how her own hands were trembling, how her stomach knotted as they got closer to Shopwells.

"They got Tom and they tried to get me. Sooner or later, they'll try again." Sherri trailed off and felt her courage waver. *Why am I doing this? Why don't I just grab my things, leave a note for Uncle Walter and Aunt Gillian and hightail it back to the city?* "We have to get in there and find whatever's controlling these chips. I'm not leaving my Uncle Walter like this."

They pulled into the Shopwells parking lot. Ben killed the headlights. The towering fluorescent lamps in the empty lot had clicked off for the night.

Sherri pointed to a line of cars moving around to the back of the store. "Look. Follow them."

They parked and watched as, one by one, the workers for the early morning shift, their neon orange vests glowing in the darkness, stepped out of their cars and trudged toward the rear door. Everyone walked with the heavy-footed gait that made them look half asleep. The worker at the front of the pack produced a swipe card and held it to a reader on the side of the door. A glowing red light flashed green and the workers stepped inside, one by one.

"We have to go. Now!" Sherri said.

Sherri and Ben crouched low, darted between the cars and caught the heavy metal door before it swung closed behind the last worker. They were in a dim concrete room stacked with boxes. The line of workers made its way through a narrow corridor. Each of them paused to slide their time cards through a scanner. A laminated poster next to the scanner read: MIND YOUR DOWNTIME! BREAK TIME IS SHOPWELLS' TIME TOO!

"Where are we?" Ben whispered.

"Looks like some kind of warehouse," Sherri said, following the other workers a few paces behind. "It's not the same place I was last time. We've got to get to the management offices. Let's duck over here and slip out when everyone's gone."

But at that moment, the heavy metal door behind them slammed closed again and a new line of workers shuffled in, sandwiching Ben and Sherri between them as they moved in unison out onto the sales floor.

"Change of plans," Sherri whispered.

They stepped through a set of swinging doors. A sign posted on the inside read: SMILE SHOPWELLS WORKERS! YOU'RE ON! The store was oddly quiet, except for the shuffling steps of the workers. Although the overhead lights were dimmed, Sherri realized where they were.

"Follow me," she whispered. She motioned toward the front of the store. But the moment they moved to slip out of line, a familiar voice called to them.

"Excuse me?"

Sherri stopped and turned back. Tony stood there, wearing an orange vest and a vacant look. Behind him, the other employees had dutifully stopped too.

Ben's eyes bulged. "Tony?"

Sherri gripped Ben's hand and squeezed. "No," she whispered.

"Morning orientation is this way," Tony said. "It's mandatory."

"Orientation, sure," Sherri said, stepping back into line. "Sorry, we're new. It's our first day."

Tony smiled, placidly. "Mine too. But remember, when we all move in the same direction, the company runs smoothly."

They marched to the centre of the store, and the group fanned out into a semicircle facing the darkened cafeteria. Sherri caught Ben's eye and slowly, slowly, one step at a time, they weaved their way backward through the crowd.

*What now?* Ben mouthed.

"Let's try to slip away while they're distracted," Sherri whispered. But she stopped when Peterson, followed closely by Rebecca, stepped through the swinging door that led to the kitchen and stood in front of the workers.

"Crap," Ben said, eyeing Peterson's tall bony frame. "He looks like a cadaver."

"Good morning, Shopwells!" Rebecca sounded like a cheerleader as she beamed at the workers. "Are we set for another exciting day?"

Rebecca's words sent a jolt of energy through the crowd. They stood straighter and clapped. "Good morning!" they said in unison.

"Before we open," Rebecca continued, "I want to make a couple of exciting announcements. First, yesterday was another record-breaking day of sales for Shopwells—thanks to all of you. Give yourselves a round of applause."

The workers hooted and hollered as if they'd been told they won the lottery.

"I'm also happy to announce that Tom Willard has reconsidered his early retirement and is back in the Shopwells fold. Tom is an invaluable member of the team, and we are so glad he decided to come home. Tom?"

Tom emerged from the kitchen. He was clean-shaven and dressed in a crisp, pressed shirt and orange tie. Despite his smile, his skin looked clammy and had a grey-green tinge to it. Sherri felt sick.

"Good morning, everyone!" Tom called in a hoarse voice. "I'm so glad to be back. I guess it says a lot about the kind of place Shopwells is. There's no other place like it, right?"

*He can say that again.*

Everyone cheered.

"But I'm not the only one making a new beginning with Shopwells," Tom said. "I'm very pleased to welcome two new staffers who are joining us for their first shifts. Could you two please come up here?"

Tony stepped forward and Sherri spotted a second worker, a woman with her black hair pulled back into a neat ponytail, who moved toward the front.

"Oh no!" Ben whispered.

"I'm sure you'll make Tony and Paula feel right at home!" Tom said, placing a hand on their shoulders. "Tony will be the kitchen supervisor for our cafeteria, and Paula here will manage the music and electronics department. Let's give a big Shopwells welcome to our new team members!"

A look of confusion passed over Tony's face. He leaned toward Tom as his foggy eyes searched the crowd. "But aren't there two other new team members?" Applause thundered.

"Uh oh," Sherri whispered. As the crowd cheered, Sherri grabbed Ben's arm and yanked him backward, around a corner and into the sporting goods aisle. They ducked behind a display of bicycle helmets.

"Did you see that? Did you see Tony and Paula?" Ben asked. Around the corner, Rebecca began to lead the crowd in a kind of singsong chant.

"Where do you go to shop well?" she called to the crowd.

"Shopwells!" they shouted back.

"I can't hear you! Where do you go to shop well?"

"Shopwells!"

"Follow me," Sherri whispered, "and stay low. While they're all having their love-in, the management offices should be wide open. Hurry!"

"Tony didn't even recognize me," Ben said.

"Ben!" Sherri hissed. "Tony's chipped. If we're going to help any of them, then we've got to move fast!"

"Okay, let's do this. You lead."

Sherri and Ben weaved through the store. They paused at the head of the sports aisle to make sure that the way was clear.

At a display of baseball equipment, Ben silently picked up two aluminum bats. He offered Sherri one. "Whack the hell out of anyone who comes near you with a chip," he said.

# CHAPTER EIGHTEEN

**SHERRI AND BEN COULD STILL HEAR REBECCA'S MORNING PEP** talk. Her voice echoed off the walls of the store.

"Here!" Sherri whispered, pushing through the door marked EMPLOYEES ONLY.

They ran up the metal staircase. When they reached the second floor, they stopped at the health clinic. Everything inside gave off a metallic gleam and smelled of corrosive cleaners. In the centre of the room stood a stark silver examination table. It looked like a slab for a corpse in the morgue. Sherri shivered.

"Jesus," Ben whispered, moving to a tray of medical instruments laid out on a crisp white towel. He reached for what looked like a pricing gun, but at its end was a large sinister-looking needle. "This must be what they use."

Sherri pictured Tom Willard, Paula and Uncle Walter being jabbed with that thing. "Take that gun," Sherri said. "And anything else that could be evidence. Check every drawer. Look for the chips."

"Where are you going?" Ben asked.

"Peterson's office. It's at the end of the hall. Meet me there. We've got five minutes, tops, then we're out of here."

She rushed down the hallway and slipped through the door marked MANAGER. PK Peterson's office was enormous, with black leather furniture and an imposing desk. She had half expected to find a wall of blinking lights and dials, like some kind of evil supercomputer. But the room was so sparsely decorated that it was almost bare.

Sherri made for Peterson's computer. Leaning the bat next to the desk, she tapped the mouse and a message popped up, asking for a password. Sherri held her breath. She typed "Lenny" into Peterson's computer. The screen went blank for a minute, and then the desktop appeared. Sherri was in.

"Dumbass," she muttered. She put the memory stick in. With a few swift clicks, she started to copy every file on the computer's hard drive. The computer whirred and a green indicator bar appeared on the screen, showing how long the files would take to be copied.

"C'mon, c'mon!"

While the files downloaded, byte by byte, Sherri rifled through Peterson's desk and the nearby filing cabinets. She looked for anything out of the ordinary.

On a side table was an iPod in a speaker dock. *What kind of music does he listen to, 'Sympathy for the Devil'?*

Sherri glanced back at the computer. It was up to fifty percent now and crawling along. *I'm running out of time. Where's Ben?* If Tony told Rebecca that he had seen them in the store, they were done. *Security might be headed this way right now.*

The computer screen showed eighty-five percent.

"Get him!" barked a voice from the hallway. Sherri grabbed her bat and started for the door. But the sound of rapid footsteps pounding down the hall stopped her in her tracks.

Sherri turned and quickly looked at the computer. The download had finished. She pulled out the memory stick, gripped the bat and ducked behind the office door. Someone burst in.

Sherri held her breath for what seemed like an eternity. The footsteps stopped.

*Please,* Sherri thought, *do not let them look at the computer.* She squeezed her eyes shut.

"And what have we here?" PK Peterson sneered, closing the door and exposing her hiding place.

Sherri swung the bat, but Peterson caught it and yanked it out of her hand. He tossed it across the office and grabbed her by the lapels of her vest. She kicked him in the shin and pulled away.

Peterson grabbed her again and spun her around. "What have you done?"

"Nothing. I was just coming to do my weekly shopping. Guess I took a wrong turn." She looked him square in the face, defiant.

"So you're the little girl who has been causing us so much trouble."

"And you're the lunatic who's been turning everyone in town into zombies." She shoved him off. Peterson stumbled backward. She ran out into the hallway.

"Stop!" Peterson's footsteps pounded behind her.

Sherri raced through the hall, down the stairs and ran through the doors onto the sales floor. The front doors were in sight.

"Get her!" Peterson yelled.

Someone grabbed Sherri from behind. Two pairs of hands

closed around her arms. Uncle Walter and Tony held her.

"Uncle Walter!" Sherri pleaded. "It's me—it's Sherri! Snap out of it! Let me go."

A crowd of workers formed around them.

"Sir?" a confused Walter asked Peterson.

"Your niece is going to join the Shopwells team," Peterson said.

"What's going on here?" Rebecca shouted, running toward them. She blanched at the sight of Sherri.

"I thought you were taking care of this problem," Peterson said, jabbing a bony finger in Sherri's direction.

The crowd of workers leaned in, peering at Sherri as if she were some sort of exotic wild animal found hiding in the store.

"I tried," Rebecca stammered. "They were supposed to take her along with Tom, but she wasn't where she was supposed to be."

"Just shows how inefficient you are," Sherri said.

"You could learn a thing or two from Rebecca," Peterson said, grinning. His mouth revealed pointed eyeteeth that gave him the look of a feral animal. "She's the model of a perfect employee. Loyal. Hard-working. Discreet. I knew as soon as I met her that she was ruthless. All I had to do was dangle enough money in front of her. Now, what were you doing in my office?" Peterson demanded.

"Decorating?" Sherri suggested.

"The time for jokes is long gone," Rebecca said. "You should have listened to me in the luncheonette. I can't help you now."

"I soooo don't need your help, lady. I know everything, so you might as well let me waltz out of here. It's over."

"Oh really?" Peterson said. "And if I were to let you go, who's going to believe your word? You'll be dismissed as some anti-corporate lunatic."

*Ben, where are you?* Sherri pictured him tucked behind an aisle, crouching low with his bat, waiting for the perfect time to strike. *Now, Ben,* she urged silently.

"Give over what you took and I'll consider letting you go." Peterson's chalky face turned red with anger as he towered over her.

She snorted. "What do you think this is—an old-fashioned spy movie? Do you think I have a secret file hidden on me? It's the new millennium," she taunted. *He'd better not search me.* "We have this thing called the internet. Your files are already safe in my inbox."

Peterson's lips curled into a snarl. "It seems you're not as clever as you think. I'll just keep you here." Peterson gripped her by the arm and yanked. "Come with me." Sherri panicked for the first time. "We'll turn you into an excellent washroom attendant," Peterson said.

"I'll have to get back to you on that. I have a couple of other offers on the table."

"You think you're brave, don't you?" Peterson said. "I suppose you're so mouthy because you think your boyfriend is coming to save you, hmm?"

Sherri stiffened. "I've never been big on the whole damsel in distress thing," she countered. "I'm quite capable of saving myself."

But she couldn't stop herself from glancing over Peterson's shoulder. *Now, Ben,* she thought, willing him to leap out from behind a display case and knock Peterson on the head.

"Your boyfriend isn't coming to save you, Miss Richmond. We've got him. In fact, he should be through the Shopwells hiring process by now."

"You're lying," Sherri said. But her courage wavered. Something told her that Peterson was not lying. They had Ben. *I should never have brought him into this.* Peterson seized her by the wrist and pulled her toward the health clinic.

Rebecca moved to follow.

"You stay here. See that everyone gets to work. We open in less than an hour."

"Yes sir," Rebecca said.

"After you." Peterson shoved her through the swinging door to the clinic. "I'm sure our technician will be happy to do another one."

Sherri's heart sank at the sight of Ben laid out on the slab. He stared at the ceiling, unblinking. He didn't move, didn't even turn to look at her.

"Davis? Davis!" Peterson called.

"He'll be right back," Ben said in a hollow-sounding voice as he slowly swung his legs off the slab and sat up. His eyes looked empty. "He told me to wait right here."

"Never mind. I can do this myself."

As Peterson strode across the room toward the chip gun on the counter, Ben caught Sherri's eye. His head twitched and he kept looking toward the open door. Sherri followed his gaze, took a step back and saw the bat leaning there.

"I've seen this done enough times," Peterson muttered to himself as he grabbed the chip gun.

Ben's body suddenly lurched and jolted as if he'd been shot through with electricity. "He'll be right back. He'll be right back. He'll be right back," Ben repeated in a robotic voice.

"Don't worry, Benjamin," Peterson said, setting down the chip gun. He dug into his pocket and pulled out what looked like the iPod from his office. "Your frequencies are just a little off. I've seen this before. I'll just tweak them and you'll feel much better. And then you can assist me with Miss Richmond here to get her settled in her new job."

As he approached Ben with the device, Sherri reached behind the door, grabbed the bat and whacked Peterson in the back of the head. The bat made a satisfying *crack*; the device flew out of his hand and he crumpled to the floor.

"Nice hit!" Ben said, leaping off the slab. "Remind me never to piss you off."

"Are you okay?" Sherri asked.

"A hell of a lot better than Davis the tech." Ben walked toward a closet in the corner and opened the door. An unconscious man in a white lab coat lay slumped there. "One hit for each of us."

"Stand back." Sherri raised the bat again and smashed the device. She swung the bat again and again until there was nothing left but a heap of twisted plastic and sparking smoking wires.

Moments later, it sounded like a stampede of horses was running up the stairs. "Oh shit, what did I do? Smashing that thing must've made the chips go haywire!"

A crowd of workers rushed in, wild-eyed and angry.

Sherri raised the bat, standing between Ben and the mob.

"What the hell's going on here?"

"Why am I here?"

"What's happening?"

"Sherri? Sherri!" It was Uncle Walter, pushing his way to the front of the crowd. He rushed to her and folded her up in a giant hug. Shocked, Sherri dropped the bat. It took her a second to hug him back.

"Uncle Walter?" She pulled away to look at him. Tears shone in his clear blue eyes.

"I'm so sorry! I knew it was you. I knew I should have helped. But I couldn't make myself move. It was like I was watching from inside someone else's body. Are you all right?"

"I'm fine! Everything's going to be fine now."

"Sherri! Ben!" Tom Willard called as he made his way to them through the crowd. "Did you do this? Did you get the chips turned off?"

Sherri nodded, a smile breaking across her face. "Looks like we did."

"Sherri did it," Ben said.

"Excuse me, excuse me!" It was Rebecca, pushing her way to the front of the crowd. "What on earth is going on in here? This is completely unacceptable. If everyone does not leave this office right away and return to the sales floor, you will receive a formal written notice for misconduct, and—"

"Stick it, lady!" called a familiar voice. It was Paula.

Rebecca blanched, glancing from Sherri, to Peterson slumped on the floor, to the hostile crowd.

Gripping Rebecca's shoulders, Sherri yanked her around so they were face to face.

"They told me it wasn't hurting anyone and I was just doing my job."

"Maybe we should put *you* out on that sales floor," said Douglas. "See how *you* like it?"

"How would you like *that*, Miss Scott?" taunted Paula.

"You took my restaurant from me!" Tony yelled.

"And my store!" shouted Anita.

Their voices rose to a deafening din.

"Tell me everything you remember. Tell me what happened," Sherri called to the crowd. "This is your chance to tell the world what they did to you."

# EPILOGUE

**BEN STOOD IN THE CRAMPED KITCHEN OF HIS TINY BASEMENT** apartment in Lewton. He stirred fresh garlic into a pot of bubbling tomato sauce and smiled as he listened to Sherri.

Sherri was giving what seemed to be her hundredth interview in the last few days. She sat at the scuffed Formica kitchen table, talking to a radio host on her cellphone. Everyone had wanted to talk to her after her exposé on the Shopwells scandal for *The Lewton Leader-Post*.

"Well I'd still like to finish my summer job up here at *The Lewton Leader-Post*," Sherri said. "My editor needs the extra help now that our municipal reporter resigned."

"That's the same reporter who was working undercover for Shopwells while you were doing your investigation?"

"Well, they're still trying to determine exactly what her role was," Sherri said. "And it will be nice to work on some stories that are a bit less—"

"Monumental?" the interviewer suggested.

"I was going to say scary," Sherri admitted. "And, after the summer, I'd still like to go to journalism school."

The interviewer laughed. "Something tells me you'll have one or two job offers coming your way."

"We'll see," Sherri said. She hadn't been prepared for the

flood of attention in the days following the Shopwells article.

Finally, the interview ended. Sherri set her phone down.

"Sorry," she said to Ben. "I promise, no more calls tonight. Nothing else will interrupt our first dinner together." She went over to the stove and hugged Ben. "That smells amazing," she said, leaning over the bubbling pot.

"Don't worry about it," Ben said, kissing her hair. "I think it's great, all this recognition. Hey, you're the reporter who broke the biggest corporate scandal of the century."

"You sound like one of the interviewers." Sherri laughed.

"Maybe I could be your press secretary?" Ben joked. He sliced brown mushrooms into a bowl. "Might be more interesting than the whole short-order cook game."

"So have you thought about what I said?" Sherri asked. "About coming back to the city with me in September and looking for a job there?"

Ben nodded and added the mushrooms to the sauce. "I think Tony will understand. I'll help him get the place back up and running. And it's not like he'll have a hard time finding a replacement. There are plenty of people looking for jobs now that Shopwells has closed down." He smiled.

Sherri's phone rang again, and she rolled her eyes.

"Last one! I promise. It could be the CBC. They were trying to schedule me in." Sherri looked at the number and frowned. Then she hit the ignore button.

"Another reporter?" Ben asked.

"No." Sherri shook her head. "It was Michael."

"Oh."

"He's left me, like, a half-dozen messages. I guess he's read all about it. He wants to come up and visit me. I never thought I'd be the kind of person to break up with someone over the phone."

Ben stirred the sauce. "You know," he said. "I think I have an idea of how to take care of this Michael situation."

"You do, do you?"

"I hung onto one of those Shopwells chip gun things."

"You did not!" Sherri gasped.

"I figure we can invite Mr. Michael over for dinner. Serve him up something nice and then—*snap!* We have a servant for life."

Sherri laughed and threw a dishtowel at him. "Not funny!"

But it was.

"C'mon, don't tell me you haven't thought of it yourself."

"Thought of what?"

"Being able to control people? Making them do whatever you want?" Ben came around the counter and took her into his arms. He kissed her eyelids, then her cheeks.

"I know what I would have you do," Sherri said, snuggling up against him.

"What's that?"

She shoved him back toward the stove. "Finish cooking dinner. I'm starving."